I am a child of the Goddess Morrigan…
I was born in the land of Éire…
And my heart blazes with its fury…
I have lived through the ages…

I seek to right those who have wronged…
I am the Maintainer of the Balance…

The Balance must be maintained

triscelle publishing

presents

madness &

reckoning

stories of the
morrigan's brood series

By

heather poinsett dunbar
& christopher dunbar

map of story locations

Éire, Alba, and Britannia
Circa 766 CE

Ómaigh

Ard Mhaca

Ard Ghlais

Caergybi

Caer Oder

Bath

London

Searoburh

Dubris

N

Not shown: Rome

Map details are on the next page. This is an excerpt from the map for Dark Alliance; some of these locations are not mentioned in Madness or Reckoning.

map guíoe

Éire, Alba, and Britannia, Circa 766 CE		
Period Name	**Modern Name**	**Modern Country**
Éire		
Ard Ghlais	Ardglass	Northern Ireland, United Kingdom
Ard Mhacha	Armagh	Northern Ireland, United Kingdom
Óghmaigh	Omagh	Northern Ireland, United Kingdom
Britannia		
Caergybi	Holyhead	Wales, United Kingdom
Caer Oder, Kingdom of Mercia	Bristol	England, United Kingdom
Bath, Kingdom of Mercia	Bath, Somerset	England, United Kingdom
Searoburh, Kingdom of Wessex	Salisbury (formerly Old Sarum)	England, United Kingdom
London, Kingdom of Mercia	London	England, United Kingdom
Dubris, Kingdom of Kent	Dover, Kent	England, United Kingdom

Note: Some of the place-names listed are not used in either Madness or Reckoning. However, this map excerpt from Dark Alliance contains most of the locations used in Madness & Reckoning. While the map is from 766 CE, the same place names may have been used in 565 CE, when both Madness and Reckoning take place. Not pictured: Rome (from Madness).

Dedication and Copyright page

For Struggling Authors Everywhere

October 2022

Madness & Reckoning

Stories of the Morrigan's Brood Series
Print ISBN-13: 978-1-937341-25-1
by Heather Poinsett Dunbar
and Christopher Dunbar
Published by Triscelle Publishing
Edited by Sarah E. Aalderink
Proofread by Jillian Rosenburg
Cover art, map, and website by Khanada Taylor
Triscelle Publishing Logo by Dayna Hartley
Original Copyright: December, 2010
Copyright © 2022 by Triscelle Publishing. All rights reserved.

Visit our website and find us on WordPress, Goodreads, Shelfari, Facebook, the Library Thing, LinkedIn, Twitter, and many other places on the Net.

www.triscellepublishing.com
triscellepublishing.wordpress.com

Also available in several eBook formats

acknowledgments

Heather's Acknowledgments

I would like to thank my husband, who breathes life into many of our creations and is endlessly patient with me. I would also like to thank our editor, Sarah (Sally), who pats my hand and tells me I've done well; Khanada, who put together the website, helped us with the layout, cover art, and interior art, which still awe me; and Dayna, who worked on a logo for us. Also, much love and thanks to my and the hub's caring circle of friends and coworkers, especially Irene, Christi, Christine, Annette, Shelley, the FList, the Fanggang, The Writer's Cabal (Vampire Division), otherwise known as Heidi, Khanada, Tracy Angelina, and Kara. In addition, I must thank my parents, who always encouraged their weirdo daughter to follow her dreams.

Christopher's Acknowledgments

I would like to thank my wife for convincing me to work with her on this novel; our editor Sarah (Sally) for nudging us on to finish this work; and my aunt Barbara for sending me that Dunbar tartan tie, which helped open my eyes to all things Celtic, historical, and mystical. I would also like to thank my parents and my wife's parents, as well as my friends and coworkers, for being so supportive in Heather's and my efforts to write our story. May the balance be maintained!

Lines of Blood-Drinkers

Algul – An Arabic blood-drinker, created by their God of War, Verethragna. Their known abilities include the power to create visual hallucinations in both mortals and other immortals. However, their vulnerability lies in strong smells. Their numbers are small, due to a genocidal war between themselves and the remnants of the Ekimmu.

Deargh Du – An ancient line of blood-drinkers from Éire (Ireland) that trace their ancestry to the Goddess Morrigan. Their true talents lie in their magical skills and their fae-like beauty, known as glamoury. They can fly, create glowing light, heal mortals as well as other immortals, and draw down darkness and shadow. Their major weakness is the metal gold. After the creation of the Ekimmu Cruitne, the Deargh Du withdrew back to their native land and ceased interacting with other blood-drinking races.

Ekimmu – A group of blood-drinkers originating in Assyria from Zaltu, God of Strife. They grew in strength and power, eventually dominating the Middle East. However, other races, such as their enemies the Algul and the Lamia, began to hunt them down, decimating their population.

Ekimmu Cruitne – The Ekimmu, fleeing a genocidal war, removed themselves to the northern regions of Alba (Scotland). After meeting some of the Deargh Du, who traveled with the Scoti tribe, an Ekimmu and a Deargh Du conspired to tip the Balance by creating a new being. Morrigan, in Her rage, sought to confine them to their lands. Ekimmu Cruitne are struck by illness whenever they try to cross the ocean. Their greatest talent is their olfactory sense, making them excellent trackers. They can also heal others, fly, read minds, and enjoy manipulating games of chance. In addition, they can create the sensation of pleasure as well as harm in themselves and their victims.

Lamia – According to legend, Lamia was a Queen of Libya who seduced Zeus. In retribution, Hera killed all Her children. Heartbroken, Lamia began feeding on the people of Greece, and before long, she had many new immortal children. The Lamia infiltrated Roman society, and soon Rome became their seat of power. The Lamia's skills lie in mind-bending, or manipulation. They even have an ability to enter dreams and manipulate the dreamer.

Ouphe – An ancient Saxon line of blood-drinkers that moved into Britannia during the Saxon conquest. Their strength is in their monstrous lycanthropic nature; many blood-drinking races can die from the wounds given by an Ouphe. Yet, the Ouphe are severely affected by silver. Their origin is a mystery.

Strigoi – A line of blood-drinkers that began from a cursed Greek beauty named Iris. Aphrodite's curse did not grant Iris and her victim's immortality until later. Yet, they only survive fifty years after their transformation. The Strigoi are telepathic and unleash uncontrollable madness upon mortals and immortals alike. Affected mortals tear at their eyes and puncture their eardrums to escape the onslaught of sights and sounds. Despite their talents, Strigoi are physically weak, stunted, and are the ugliest of the blood-drinkers.

Sugnwr Gwaed – A British group of blood-drinkers created by Cernunnos, the Horned God of animals, wilderness, and the wild hunt. Their strengths include enhanced communication with animals and their talent for vocal persuasion. They can convince their victims of almost anything. They also fly, like the other Celtic lines, and have an aptitude for healing others.

Chiang-Shih – A Chinese line of blood-drinkers that originated from Shenlong, a dragon God. Shenlong created the Chiang-Shih to protect His earthly treasures from greedy mortals. While the Chiang-Shih can control storms like Shenlong, they can only fly when the moon is full and have difficulty crossing water. Little else is known about them, as they chose not to interact with most of the western lines.

Pacu Pati – Blood-drinkers from India that originated from Kali. The Pacu Pati tend to cloister themselves with their new families of other Pacu Pati and do not often meet with the other lines. When other lines have witnessed the celebrations of the cycles of life and death, they tend to misunderstand the celebrations, and a lack of a common language generally adds to the confusion.

Other lines will be revealed in future works.

character and pronunciation guide

Key Character Backgrounds and Pronunciations	
Madness	
Mandubratius	**Awvarwy** (*a-war-wee*)

As a co-consul of the Lamia, the former self-proclaimed Chieftain of the Trinovantes failed to acquire the prize, bringing shame to the once great empire. From the confines of his demented mind, Mandubratius must find a way to come to grips with his failure or risk being executed by a loyal steward of the empire.

Tertia Amata Antonia	**Amata**

What a dutiful co-consul to Mandubratius and the Lamia is Amata, one of few women in the Senatorial class of the Lamia. Even following Mandubratius' failure to grab the Phallus Maximus, Amata stays true to her former plaything - who shares with her the same sponsor, Felician - but at what price?

Felician (*Not his real name*)	**Felician**

Few living Lamia truly know how much they have to thank Felician for shaping the Lamia into what it is today. Even those he sponsored, Amata and Mandubratius, have no clue as to his true purpose... too bad they conspired to execute him on the floor of the Lamia Senate. Pity.

Patroclus Statilius Messalinus	**The Legate**

Once a legate under Emperor Trajan, Patroclus now serves the Lamia co-consul as their advisor, bodyguard, and problem solver. However, his loyalty is first to the Lamia. Should either co-consul stray, he would rectify the situation.

Reckoning	
Sáerlaith Ní Adhamdh	**Sáerlaith** (*saer-la*)

This new leader of the Deargh Du Council of Five must follow Morrigan's path in order to bring balance to the Deargh Du, but even Her path is wrought with peril, and a misstep may lead to the dissolution of the Deargh Du.

Máire Ní Conghal (*ex Maél Muire*)	**Máire** (*moya*)

Formerly Chieftain of the Uí Máine of Béal Átha an Fheadha, Máire, a Deargh Du, finds herself in the midst of political intrigue, as she must decide whether to follow Marcus, her Father-in-Darkness, or Sáerlaith, the leader of the Council of Five.

Marcus Galerius Primus Helvetticus	**Marcus**

Formerly a general and Praetor of Gaul under Gaius Julius Caesar, Marcus became a Deargh Du and led their armies against the invading Lamia. With the war over, Marcus must decide how far he will go to help Sáerlaith maintain the Balance.

Sive Uí Fergus Uí Máine	**Aunt Sive** (*se-ve*)

Widow of Fergus Mac Aerlon Uí Máine, who was murdered by Lamia, and aunt to Maél Muire, who is now a Deargh Du and bears the name 'Máire', Sive must carry on the traditions of old, living a lonely existence that she does not deserve.

Aisling Ní Dáithí Uí Feidlimid	Aisling (*ASH-ling*)

This direct blood descendant of Adhamdh, the Mílesian king who became the first Deargh Du, must decide whether to follow her heart or follow her Father-in-Darkness, Conlan. Or perhaps events will make the decision for her.

Claudius Metrius Sertorius	Claudius

Originally a lieutenant under General Marcus Galerius Primus Helvetticus, Claudius later became a Sugnwr Gwaed. Claudius has become quite bored, since fighting alongside Marcus and Mac Alpin against the Lamia. Though he would never admit to it, Claudius misses the company of his companions.

Arwin Mac Alpin	Mac Alpin

Once the scourge of the Romans, Arwin Mac Alpin, an Ekimmu Cruitne, has won nary a game of chance against his fellow Ekimmu Cruitne. If only he could find some excuse to reunite with Marcus and Claudius, those chumps, and win once more.

Seosaimhín Uí Turrlough Uí Niall	Seosaimhín (*sho-siv-een*)

As she watches that soulless one, Maél Muire, the bride, rip the heart of her son, the groom, from his chest while standing at the alter during their wedding, Seosaimhín manages to place a strong curse upon the murderer. Will this curse cause the eternal pain and suffering that the wielder wishes, or will the curse fade with the passage of time? Perhaps soon, the opportunity will arise to bring justice to that soulless one, and to all of her kin.

Other Character Name Pronunciations

Bearach	*ba-rax*	Caile	*kay-la*

Irish Story and Welsh Location Pronunciations

Ard Ghlais	*ord glass*	Cill Ala	*kill-la-la*
Ard Mhacha	*ord wa-hcah*	Loch Dá Chaoch	*lo-hc daoh-hco*
Béal Átha an Fheadha	*beh-lo-ina*	Loch Garman	*lo-hc gar-mon*
Béal Easa	*bell-assa*	Mhuine Chonalláin	*moonie hahn-alon*
Brú na Bóinne	*bruna bun-ee-ay*	Ráth Cruachan	*raw kroo-uh-ckahn*
Ómaigh	*oh-mah*	Caergybi	*car-ger-bee*

gods and goddesses of the series

Irish Pantheon – Tuatha dé Danann (People of Dana)	
Aine (*An-ya*)	*Goddess of love and fertility*
Aongas Og (*An-gus Og*)	*God of love and youth*
Brigid (*Bri-jid*)	*Goddess of healing, writing, water, and cats*
Dagda (*Dah-dah*)	*The 'good' God of many skills*
Dana (*Day-na*)	*The Mother Goddess*
Lugh (*Loo*)	*Multi-skilled God of battle, light, writing, and the harvest*
Medb (*May-v*)	*Goddess of sovereignty*
Manannán Mac Lir (*Mannan-awan Mac Lir*)	*Guide to the Otherworld and God of the wind, travels, sea, and sailing*
Morrigan (*Mor-ee-gan*)	*Goddess of death, battle, blood, and rebirth*
Nuada (*Nu-a-da*)	*God of healing and weaponry*
British Pantheon	
Cernunnos	*God of animals, wilderness, fertility, and the Wild Hunt*
Greek / Roman Pantheon	
Aphrodite (*af-rə-dy-tee*) / Venus ('wɛnʊs)	*Goddess of love, beauty, and sexuality / Goddess of love, beauty, and fertility*
Ares (áreːs) / Mars (*Mārs*)	*God of War and Manly Virtues / God of War; part of the Archaic Triad*
Hera (*Hēra*) / Juno ('juːnoː)	*Queen of the Gods and Goddess of marriage, women and birth / Patron Goddess of Rome and Goddess of women; part of the Capitoline Triad*
Zeus (*Zews*) / Jupiter (*Joo-pi-ter*)	*King of the Gods and God of the sky, thunder, lightning, law, order, and justice / King of the Gods and God of the sky and thunder; part of the Capitoline Triad; Patron Deity of Rome*
Arabic (Zoroastrian) Pantheon	
Verethragna	*God of war and sexual potency*
Assyrian Pantheon	
Zaltu (*Zal-too*)	*God of strife*
Hindu Pantheon	
Kali (*Kālī*)	*Goddess of time and change; "She who destroys"; "Redeemer of the Universe"*
Chinese Pantheon	
Shenlong (*shén lóng*)	*A dragon god in Chinese mythology known as the "Master of Storms"*

madness

a story of the morrigan's brood series

By

heather poinsett dunbar
& christopher dunbar

Madness takes place after the events of Crone of War:
Morrigan's Brood Book II and before Dark Alliance:
Morrigan's Brood Book III. All events take place during
565 CE in ancient Rome.

Rome, 565 CE

"Spring brings life to the land. Then summer comes and sees it grow to its fullest. Then in autumn, we harvest all ideas. All die in winter, and then the sun is reborn and all begins anew in spring."

Patroclus stared down at Mandubratius, resisting the urge to kill the co-consul for mercy's sake.

Mandubratius had remained in bed for the greater part of a year, and when he did not sleep or feed, he babbled nonsense, sometimes in Latin, sometimes in Gaelic, and sometimes in that peculiar tongue, the name of which Patroclus could not recall, the Britons used over five centuries ago.

The legate studied the opulent surroundings of Mandubratius' hidden room, noting that the sweet scent of frankincense had been replaced with the odor of foul medicines.

The danger of suspicious senators discovering the co-consul's condition increases every night he remains in seclusion.

"Shhhh," Amata shushed as she applied a compress to Mandubratius' forehead. She turned towards Patroclus and the elder Lamia physician, who tended Mandubratius' condition. "This should have worked," she complained, directing a glare towards the old blood-drinker.

Iason, the physician, stared down at Mandubratius and leaned in, before spreading the co-consul's eyes open.

It seems somewhat absurd that a Lamia would need the ministrations of a physician, and the treatment processes being employed seem rather pointless.

"Let us wait a moment, co-consul, before you pass judgment," Iason said.

"The tortoise formation is executed by a centurion giving the order of 'testudo' and then–" babbled Mandubratius.

"It does not appear that he's improving as a result of your latest treatment," Amata interjected, interrupting Mandubratius, as she glared at Iason.

The physician raised his hands. "Perhaps we have not given the treatment enough time," he suggested.

"I've reached my limit with this inept physician," Patroclus growled. "Clearly, none of your treatments have worked!" Patroclus exclaimed as he fixed his gaze on Iason, desiring to kill that little man.

"Patroclus, do not be so judgmental," Amata yelled at him, baring her teeth. Her eyes glowed red, revealing her Lamia nature.

"No, this has gone on too long. We need… I need Mandubratius up!"

"I will repeat what I told you before I started treating our co-consul," Iason pleaded as he backed away a few steps. "I do not know what ails him. As a rule, we Lamia do not suffer illnesses of the body. With this last treatment, I've been able to conclude that this is not an ailment of the body. This ailment rests in Mandubratius' mind, and I'm not skilled in treating illnesses of this kind. However, there is a Lamia physician who can."

"Who?" Amata asked, after rising from her place next to Mandubratius.

"I don't know his real name," Iason admitted. "We just called him Kosmos. He was a student of Hippocrates."

"Then, bring him here," Amata ordered.

Patroclus tried to remember whether he knew this Kosmos, and then he recalled that his intelligence network had informed him that Mandubratius and Amata associated in private with many of the aged, Greek Lamia who remained in hiding from others of their line in Rome.

"Very well... I will seek him out. However, he's not in Rome, so it may take a few nights," Iason admitted with a slight shrug.

"Just find him," Patroclus demanded. "More than your reputation is at stake." He stared at the physician and watched fear register in the other Lamia's eyes.

The elder Lamia left, scurrying out of the room.

Amata sighed, sat down next to Mandubratius, and stroked his dark hair.

Mandubratius continued spewing madness-addled sentences, but Patroclus soon realized there might be some meaning to the co-consul's gibberish. "Beast with a banshee scream pummels the young man and takes his breath and the very beating of his heart," Mandubratius continued.

"Poor Awvarwy," cooed Amata, breaking the legate's concentration.

Patroclus felt some shock at hearing the old name.

Amata smiled at Patroclus as she took one of Mandubratius' hands.

"So much of what he says seems meaningless," Patroclus considered aloud for Amata's benefit, as he wrestled with the notion that the co-consul might be trying to communicate with them. "Yet, I wonder..." He stepped over to Amata and stared down at Mandubratius' half-opened eyes. "Sometimes, what he says seems truly random, and at other times, it seems to be true communication," he commented.

Amata looked up at Patroclus. Her blue eyes seemed to turn violet. "Do you think we will be able to cure him?" she asked.

"Yes, we will," he lied, in hopes of soothing Amata's nerves. Patroclus secretly feared that they would be trapped with Mandubratius in this condition forever, unless they made the decision to kill Mandubratius and end his suffering.

chapter one

wvarwy felt a little disoriented. At first, he could discern no sights, smells, or sounds, but soon he began to hear harp music and smell wood smoke, cooking meats, and mead. As the harp music swelled, Awvarwy opened his eyes and saw that he stood in a simple, yet clean hall. As the odor of wood smoke indicated, a fire roared in the hearth.

The light from the hearth and from the oil lamps that hung around this simple hall revealed to Awvarwy that he stood within his home. Familiar faces regarded him, but he struggled to remember their names. Soon, uplifting music drew him away from those faces. He nearly choked in emotion as he witnessed the fingers of his wife, Anna, glide over the strings of her harp. He lifted his arm to gesture at her, only to discover his hand held a cup of mead.

This event seems so very familiar, and yet so different. I always held feasts at my home. This must be a feast from my past, but from when…

As Anna stopped playing and the song came to an end, his guests sipped at their drinks, and then everyone began to clap.

Awvarwy joined in their applause and smiled at Anna.

Her returned smile curved up into a mischievous grin as she strolled over to him with her harp in hand.

He pulled her in close and kissed her, though the embrace felt awkward, with her holding her harp between them. Awvarwy felt relief when a servant took her harp.

Free of her burden, Anna hugged Awvarwy with both arms. Soon, her hands strayed from his back, and he released her from his embrace. "My song, was it pleasing?" she whispered. Her eyes exuded doubt and unease, as if she questioned the quality of her music.

"Your music is always so moving," he admitted.

No other harpist plays with as much skill and emotion as my wife.

Anna smiled again and said, "I remembered you had much fondness for this song, Awvarwy." She kissed him on his left cheek, but afterwards, she left his company.

Their guests surrounded her, offering her praises for her music.

As Awvarwy watched her take a cup of mead from another servant, a shadow fell across his face, and Awvarwy turned his head to look upon the source of that shadow.

A man stood before him, and Awvarwy recognized him as being his old friend, Gaelen. Gaelen walked up to Awvarwy, patted his shoulder, and said, "I truly appreciate this hospitality, my friend, but I fear the hour is late. I must retire. Tomorrow, I shall return to the fish."

Awvarwy's senses felt strong again.

I must have fallen asleep during Anna's song.

Awvarwy shrugged his confusion aside and embraced Gaelen, hoping he did not seem out of sorts. "I'm always happy to share what is mine with my neighbors."

Gaelen returned the hug before releasing him. "Have you seen Gwynfor?"

Awvarwy soon recalled that Gaelen's son bore that name.

"I watched Gwynfor and Mabon join the other children earlier in a hurling match," *Anna interjected after finishing her drink.* "I'll go find your son and ours."

Mabon... Mabon was... is my son's name.

Awvarwy's heart felt heavy as he contemplated seeing his son again.

He watched his wife leave their home, trying not to ignore the gracious well wishes of his guests, but Anna's words outside to the lands distracted him.

She soon returned, looking worried. "I can't find either of them," *Anna said, rubbing her hands together, as a cold wind chilled the air outside.*

"They are probably just playing," *he suggested.* "We shall look for them. Gaelen can go east, you can go west, and I'll go south into the forest. We'll find them." *He took Anna's hands and smiled. For some reason, he felt a strange contentment as he held his wife's hands.* "Come... the boys couldn't have gone far."

Gaelen passed out torches to the remaining members of the family and servants.

"When you find them, ring the bell in the middle of the village once as a signal to let the others know to return," *he instructed everyone.*

Awvarwy watched the search party leave before departing his home. He began to meander through the forest. "Gwynfor? Mabon!" *he called, hearing the boys' names echo through the rest of the village.*

He wandered down the hunting path, grateful for the light of the torch and a clear trail. After walking about a hundred paces, a light mist grew and began to obscure the path through the forest.

His toe found a solid rock or root. "By the Gods," *Awvarwy swore, in pain. He lowered himself to the ground, first to massage his injured toe, but while on the ground, he decided to attempt to find the boys' tracks in the dirt, assuming they had come this way. Then a strange sensation gripped him, and he looked up at the forest crown.*

The trees and plants seemed different, somehow. A bright light grew in the east, and he wondered how the sun could be rising now, since it had recently set.

Or so I thought. Could I have walked all night?

Awvarwy turned in the opposite direction on the path in order to return home, hoping that the others had found the boys by now, though he had not heard the signal bell. As he walked, the mist began to fade, and his path grew clear, but the strange passage of time worried him.

The sun began to climb to its zenith, though it had not been long since dawn had kissed the night.

After I get home, I will speak to Meilyr about this strange occurrence. The druid must know something, of use.

He continued walking to the north, when he realized that he approached a grove. He stopped at the edge and wondered how long it had been since the druids had last tended it, for vines, unchecked by sickles, extended throughout the trunks and branches, choking them, and the ground lay littered with detritus.

Awvarwy first walked the circumference of the grove, speculating on the diseased trees surrounding the stone altar in the center, but when he approached the center altar, he felt unease, and the smell of death washed over him. Awvarwy exhaled, trying to find clean air.

Why do I feel this strange foreboding? Death is a natural part of life.

He continued walking without purpose, staring at the decay around him, when the firm ground became soft, creating a sucking noise whenever Awvarwy planted or lifted a foot. He looked at his feet and realized that he stood in a muddy puddle of blood. He followed the blood pool with his eyes and noticed that it came from the top of the center altar stone.

With effort, he sloshed toward the altar, taking care not to lose his footing on this blood-soaked ground. When Awvarwy arrived at the altar, he noticed that the top stone still held a large pool of vitae, which continued to pour in streams to the ground.

No small animal sacrifice could have produced so much vitae.

Awvarwy shuddered in horror as he realized that this blood came not from an animal, but from a human. He backed away, fearful that whoever committed this act watched him even now.

He noticed light glinting off a metallic object in the grass. Curiosity overcame his concerns that malicious eyes watched him, and so he began walking towards the glimmering metal.

A silvered blade reflected sunlight back to him.

He crept to the glowing radiance and found the blade, despite it being somewhat obscured by the grass. He knelt onto the ground, picked up the knife, and held it up to study it. "You're no druid's scythe or boline," Awvarwy spoke aloud.

Without warning, a noise in the distance startled him, and Awvarwy looked up from his crouch and parted the grass so he could spot the source of the noise.

He spied a large, green-eyed black cat staring at him from the edge of the grove.

The cat crouched towards the earth, flicking its tail back and forth, as it gazed at Awvarwy with ever steady eyes. It began to slink towards him, allowing its belly to remain close to the ground. While the grass obscured its approach, the cat's tail remained elevated above the tall blades. After a few seconds passed, the cat stopped five feet away from Awvarwy and began sniffing the ground.

Awvarwy's curiosity grew as the cat continued examining the ground with great intensity. Now, with the cat so close, Awvarwy had greater opportunity to study it.

With the exception of a few small white hairs, the cat's gleaming black coat reminded Awvarwy of a moonless midnight.

It seems much larger than most of the cats that live in the village, but despite its size, it appears fit and muscular.

The cat raised his head and began to approach him again.

Awvarwy could see that it held something in its mouth.

The black cat stopped a few inches away from Awvarwy before dropping something shiny at his feet. The cat then stared up at Awvarwy as if it were a hunting dog presenting him with a trophy.

Awvarwy crawled forward from his crouch to examine what the cat had dropped. He picked up what appeared to be a bracelet and began to examine it. Then, he noticed several drops of blood glistening from its shiny surface.

Mother loved this bracelet...

Awareness hit him, as Awvarwy realized...

I am holding my mother's bracelet!

As he stood up in haste, he dropped the jewelry from his nervous fingers.

Wait... I remembered this place, now. I saw something here, somewhere in my past, but I wanted to forget every shred of this memory. I just want to be at home, absent this memory.

His fear grew, as bits and pieces of this fearful remembrance fused together against his will.

"You must acknowledge what happened, Awvarwy," cooed a feline voice in his head. "Scream, and you'll feel better."

Awvarwy screamed as he opened his eyes wide, but all he could see was Amata's worried face staring down at him.

The grove, the cat, and the bracelet had disappeared...

Nothing more than a distant dream.

chapter two

"Can you hear me, Awvarwy?"

Mandubratius' screaming ceased, but his eyes remained focused on hers. He began to blink, but soon he stared up at Amata again, though this time, his madness seemed to abate.

"Amata," he whispered, "where am I?"

"We're at the temple in Rome," she informed him, hoping he would understand that much at least.

"Strange," he said, his voice growing in strength. "A moment ago, I was elsewhere."

"Awvarwy," she whispered, "you've been here, in a delusional state, for over a year."

"But I was in Bryttania... Britannia," he countered. "I was at home with my wife and our children, the neighbors came by for a feast, and my wife regaled them with her enchanting harp playing."

Amata leaned over and stroked his hair again. "That was a dream. It wasn't real." She worried that he would slip back into his delusional state.

Mandubratius reached up, touched the left side of her face, and yelled in a frantic tone, "But I was there!"

Amata forced herself to settle her mind. "Calm yourself, Awvarwy. I am telling you that you've been here all this time."

Mandubratius lowered his hand, but he continued to stare at her, confusion and disbelief evident on his face. "How can that be?" His eyes darted away from her, towards his feet. "Why am I in bed?"

"Because you were... unwell," Amata informed him, surprised that he seemed more coherent than he had been since madness had engulfed him.

"What ailment could have kept me abed for over a year?" he asked, though he seemed more composed than a moment ago.

"I told you that you were delusional. You were experiencing fits of madness," Amata repeated.

Mandubratius stared up at her again. "You really do have beautiful eyes."

She realized then that he still might be a bit crazed, but at least he could speak with her now. The belief that his torment might finally be at an end caused her to weep. "Oh, Awvarwy," Amata whispered, as she rubbed her forehead.

"'Awvarwy'?" Mandubratius continued to stare at her. "You don't usually call me by my given name." He began to push himself up into a sitting position.

She scooted closer to him and helped him sit upright.

He shook his head a little. "So, I've been delusional for a year. How... what happened to me, Amata?"

She felt her concern grow. "How could you not remember?" she asked. She felt her words turn sharp.

"Please don't get angry with me," Mandubratius retorted, before resting his elbows against his raised knees.

"I'm not angry," Amata cooed in what she hoped was a calming voice. She took a deep breath before continuing. "I'm just worried." She closed her eyes for a moment and then opened them. "Perhaps it's best that you don't remember what transpired." She rested her hands on his shoulders.

Mandubratius shrugged away her grip on him. "I want to remember what happened. Why would I not want to remember?" His eyes began to turn red.

Amata rose from her seat and grabbed a chair, before scooting it closer to Mandubratius' bed. She sat down and stared at him for a moment, noting how he continued to lock eyes with her in a demanding way. "Because, Awvarwy, I'm afraid if you remember, what happened to you before will happen again."

His expression changed from fierce command to pained confusion, and his hands moved to his knees. His emotional state seemed to change from confusion to self-doubt and fear. Mandubratius looked away from Amata and began staring at the far wall.

She knew he needed some reassurance, now, so she sidled closer and then placed a hand on his. "Awvarwy, look at me," she demanded in a subtle tone, though his eyes remained locked on the opposite end of room. "Mandubratius, look at me," she ordered in the same tone and manner that Felician used when speaking to Mandubratius. She forced herself into her oldest friend's head and visualized their sponsor. Amata felt her mouth open in shock as Mandubratius pushed aside his blankets, rolled his legs off the bed, and stood up at attention.

"Yes, sponsor," Mandubratius acknowledged in the clipped tone of a military subordinate.

She had doubted her manipulation skills, and yet he responded. "Very good," she congratulated, while continuing the manipulation. "A special physician will arrive soon to treat your medical condition."

Mandubratius nodded.

"Until he arrives, I want you to sleep. Get back in bed, and either Patroclus or I will awake you when it is time to rise."

"I shall obey." Mandubratius then sat down and reclined in the bed.

Amata restrained herself from assisting him with the covers.

Felician would never do such a thing for Mandubratius.

Amata glanced at her co-consul and saw his eyes flutter and then shut. She felt relief that her attempt succeeded. Amata stood and pulled open the door.

Perhaps Patroclus has news about this Kosmos.

Patroclus sat at his desk in the office within the catacombs, hating his administrative duties.

Someone has to administer the Lamia. Amata always says that my talents allow me to complete my duties quickly and without the mistakes that others typically make. Of course, that Amata has no head for paperwork, so all these tasks fall to me anyway.

Despite the efficiency he applied to administering the Lamia, Patroclus still heard the whispers, from time to time, breathed by those who showed a growing desire to take over the governance of the Lamia.

I wonder whether a usurper would enjoy all the work that comes with governance. Their complaints are not surprising. After all, they have not seen Mandubratius in well over a year.

Patroclus closed his eyes, contemplating the games that continued to be played to maintain the illusion of governance without the presence of one of their leaders. When he opened his eyes, Patroclus noticed Amata staring at him from the chair on the opposite side of his desk. "Where have you been?" he demanded.

"You know very well where I've been," she snapped at him. Amata lowered her eyes and began to redden, even though he doubted that she had fed in the last few hours. "Please, forgive my rudeness," she apologized.

He felt his own flash of guilt for his earlier annoyance with her, but he decided not to reply and just gazed at her.

"Have you heard from Iason or Kosmos?" Amata asked.

"No," he answered. "Iason left immediately, so I hope he will arrive soon."

As Amata nodded her head, her dark hair became a veil, covering her eyes, for a moment.

"I'm not sure how much longer the senate will accept our excuses regarding your co-consul," Patroclus stated.

Amata's eyes her locked on his. "What do you mean? Has something happened?" she queried, her voice rising in volume.

Sometimes I worry she might become as crazed as Mandubratius.

"I'm not sure, but if someone listens…" he whispered, before motioning for Amata to draw closer. After Amata moved towards him, Patroclus continued whispering. "There is a rumor that the senators wish to select new consuls."

Amata frowned. "Are you shirking your duties, Legate?"

"No!" he shouted. "It is you who is not doing your job! I'm doing your job and the Briton's job as well! I'm not a consul, and I never wished to become one. My authority is not recognized, you realize. You must show your face at the senate instead of playing nurse."

Amata lowered her eyes again. "That may be possible, now," she suggested. "I was going to tell you sooner, but Mandubratius is awake and coherent, at least he was awake, until I coaxed him into slumber."

Patroclus felt his spirits rise. "He is? Why didn't you say this first?"

Amata raised her eyes to his.

He felt a little fear as he witnessed her annoyed glare.

"Because you wouldn't let me have my say," she spat.

Patroclus closed his mouth, calmed himself, and continued. "Well, now you can have your say. How is he? Do we still need this special physician?"

Amata leaned back and crossed her arms over her chest. "He spoke, but I think he's still somewhat affected by his madness."

He felt compelled to ask how she knew this.

"He doesn't remember what happened," she added.

"What does he not remember?" Patroclus asked, afraid of the possible answer.

She glared at him, annoyance present in her features. "How could he know what he doesn't remember, Patroclus? I'm not going to ask!" she growled.

He felt confused.

"If he remembers what happened, he could be lost to us again. Even worse, if he does remember, he might insist on returning to Éire and finding the real Phallus Maximus. You know as well as I do that our army is decimated!"

Patroclus nodded. "I agree. It seems that the best option is to keep Mandubratius sedated until Kosmos arrives. I will stay with him so you can speak with the senate if needed."

Amata smiled. "You know, you are the only person I would trust with Awvarwy's care."

He wondered whether she should trust him at all, with Mandubratius alone and unprotected. Instead of filling her with doubt, Patroclus met her stare and stated, "The honor is to serve," wondering whether she knew of his desire to do away with the co-consul if his state did not improve... soon.

andubratius exhaled, reveling in his relaxation. He thought once no baths could compare with those in Rome. However, Byzantium, with its warmer climate, proved better than he believed it could be.

Julian will win this battle against the Persians, and this victory will elevate the emperor's power and influence.

Mandubratius closed his eyes and soaked up the warm currents of the bath.

If I desire it, the slaves will bring wine, prostitutes, and even blood.

The last few years had been most pleasurable. Mandubratius had shaped and formed Julian like clay between his fingers. Part of Mandubratius wished he had travelled to Persia with the emperor's army.

If only Felician could witness this triumph, yet my foolish sponsor remains in Rome. Perhaps I will call for a prostitute...

The warm water and the promise of victory proved to be quite an aphrodisiac, but before he could call for a slave to bring him a few prostitutes, a voice as cold as ice water pierced his contentment like a dagger.

"Are you quite enjoying yourself, Mandubratius, or are you using that loathsome name your barbaric parents gave you when your mother squeezed you out of her often plowed loins?"

Mandubratius shivered, but he hoped Felician had not witnessed his surprise. With as much nonchalance as he could muster, he opened his eyes and watched the other Lamia slide into the bath, opposite of him.

"Oh, this is quite wonderful," his sponsor purred.

"This is indeed a surprise. I didn't expect you here, Sponsor." Mandubratius did his best to bury his shock, as Felician would exploit any hint of weakness.

Felician stretched in the water. "I didn't think that you liked hot water, as I seem to remember your preference for ice-covered streams."

Mandubratius waited, since Felician still had not made eye contact.

His sponsor leaned back against the wall of the bath.

Mandubratius concentrated his senses on the others within the building to see whether other Lamia had accompanied his sponsor, yet he perceived nothing but mortals... for now, at least.

"For some reason, I doubt you were expecting me. I think this is your attempt to hide your surprise. If you were expecting me, you would not be alone and naked in a bath house, would you?" Felician asked.

Mandubratius attempted to steady himself without revealing his unsteadiness.

"You make it sound as if I should fear you."

"Fear me?" Felician asked, false incredulity in his tone.

Mandubratius wondered whether he should risk asking his sponsor what was on his mind.

Why is he here?

Mandubratius continued to ask himself that question deep within the recesses of his mind, though fearful that Felician could eavesdrop on his more protected thoughts. "Have I done anything that would compel you to travel to Byzantium?" Mandubratius cringed inside, afraid that his sponsor would strike him, but instead, Felician smiled.

"Awvarwy, Awvarwy, Awvarwy... Gods below, I hate that name. It's so ... clumsy and foreign. Awvarwy, when I first found you, I did not plan to sponsor you... I merely wanted to drain you dry, despite the fact that there was so little vitae left in you. Even if I had been seeking out new Lamia to sponsor, I simply would not have felt that any Briton could have risen to prominence in the Lamia, but Amata wanted a toy, and I owed her..."

Mandubratius wondered how Felician was indebted to Amata.

"... so I sponsored you and trained you. I spent centuries training you, and then you rewarded my charity with betrayal."

Mandubratius noticed his sponsor's cold blue eyes begin to turn red. He felt like arguing with Felician, but Mandubratius knew it would be best to remain silent.

Felician has beaten that fact into me many times, over the years.

Felician did not blink, so Mandubratius' dread grew as he considered the possible reasons why his sponsor had come here.

"There was a time when you did not know when to hold your tongue, and I would have struck you for such behavior. So, Mandubratius, I shall give you leave to speak. I am certain you would like to explain yourself."

Mandubratius steadied himself again. "For what reasons do I need to explain myself?" he queried, while attempting to appear calm.

Felician smashed his fist against the surface of the water, splashing them both. "You betrayed me!" his sponsor growled. Felician's eyes turned completely red, but after a moment of intense agitation, the elder Lamia regained his composure.

Mandubratius felt strange satisfaction knowing he had cracked his sponsor's calm facade.

"You sided against me. You helped that mortal... Julian... rise to power when you knew that I wanted a theocratic empire under the rule of the pope, who I control. Everything was perfect! Our wealth, power, and influence grew by leaps and bounds! Since I brought that damnable Jewish cult to Rome, the masses have remained under our domination!"

Mandubratius tried not to roll his eyes.

That cult arrived in Rome on its own, but I have to admit that Felician has a strong influence in its dogma and its corruption.

"But you had to get that… puppy to bound into power, and you convinced it to become an apostate, of all things, and reject the faith! What were you thinking, Awvarwy?"

Mandubratius remained silent and adjusted his gaze to stare at the water, instead of meeting Felician's stare. He heard Felician grumble under his breath and decided it was appropriate now to try to explain himself. "Permission to speak!" Mandubratius requested in a clipped, precise tone.

In response, Felician waved his hand in an impatient manner.

"Was I not doing what you taught me to do, to stand on my feet and gain power and influence, Sponsor? Is this not the way of the Lamia?" he asked Felician.

Felician leaned forward. "The Lamia way is to follow your Consul, who is me. You went against me, Awvarwy!" After a moment of rage, Felician resumed his calm demeanor and shut his eyes. "Well, Mandubratius, despite your digressions against me… I forgive you." Felician reopened his eyes, stared at Mandubratius, and smiled.

Mandubratius sucked in a breath as the realization dawned on him that Emperor Julian was dead.

"Yes, Julian is dead," Felician stated, as he continued to smile. "He was killed by one of his own soldiers who believed this to be a death ordained by God, although some will believe the Persians killed him."

Will Felician kill me next?

"Awvarwy, I have spent so much time training you, so I will not toss you aside for such a small inconvenience. It is just one, miniscule emperor, after all. You show much promise, but I fear that you have demonstrated you will never amount to anything. You will never accomplish more than I have. You are a failure, but I must accept some blame for that. After all, your ineptitude could be because you are a Briton."

Felician scooted over to Mandubratius and then leaned his face closer so he could stare into Mandubratius' eyes. "My only regret is that I should have killed you that fateful night on the beach in Éire. Your bath is over, and it is time for you to return to Rome. There is nothing left for you here, now."

Felician climbed out of the bath and, with his back to Mandubratius, he began to pat himself dry.

Mandubratius felt relief that Felician was unable to see the tear in his eye.

Patroclus continued walking through the tunnels of the hidden, underground levels of the temple, contemplating what could be done should Mandubratius insist on returning to Éire.

I have always followed the orders of the co-consuls since the night of the great schism, between the younger Lamia and the others who had supported Felician.

Upon reaching the door to Mandubratius' chamber, Patroclus stopped and peered at the purple-clad guards, who resembled the praetorians from centuries ago, standing in front of the door. Both guards saluted him, and so he returned the gesture.

"Has anyone tried to come up since Amata left?" Patroclus asked.

The guard to his left shook his head. "No, legate."

"Very well. Have a servant bring a pouch of blood. I'll be inside."

"Yes sir." The other guard opened the door.

As soon as Patroclus walked through, he heard the guards shut the door behind him, followed by footfalls from one of them running down the hall.

A few oil lamps and candles lit the interior of the large chamber, bathing the sleeping form of Mandubratius in yellow-orange light.

A sudden impulse compelled Patroclus to wake Mandubratius to see whether the co-consul would wake and be lucid. However, the desire faded away as he stared down at the sleeping Briton.

No one wants to return to Éire. All Lamia know, such a venture would tear us apart. To save the Lamia, Mandubratius may have to die, and I would assume the duty of executioner, if it becomes necessary, for the good of the Lamia.

The bathhouse and bath faded into mist, as did his sponsor.

Mandubratius inhaled the scents of trees, berries, and fresh dirt. He stood, clothed, in yet another grove, though this one hummed with magic and promise. Mandubratius took a few steps toward the east before hearing sounds of combat, of men and women screaming in battle, and he felt the need to run towards the fight.

"Going somewhere?"

Mandubratius stopped and turned around, looking for the familiar voice, but he could see no one who demanded words with him. Then a midnight-hued motion caught his eyes, and Mandubratius gazed upon the same black cat from his earlier vision.

"You, again." He grinned at the cat. "What are you doing here, wherever here is?" Mandubratius asked as he knelt on one knee to get a better look at the cat.

As the black cat's eyes narrowed, their brilliant, yellowed-green tinge grew deeper. "Do you not remember this place?" asked the cat, though as before, its mouth did not move.

Mandubratius rotated his head further to examine his current whereabouts.

A rich carpet of green grass extended through the grove, and a wet mist infused the air.

He felt the sensation of enchantment grow within himself. Soon, a memory swelled within his brain. "I'm in Éire, aren't I?"

"Yes," the cat purred, "but where and when?"

The noise of battle commands echoed through the grove and began to increase. The sights and sounds dredged up a name.

"This is Mhuine Chonalláin during our battle with the Celtic lines," he answered. Then, Mandubratius stretched his right hand to the cat.

The feline stuck out his nose for a sniff before rubbing himself against the outstretched hand. "Very good," the cat murmured. The animal then tensed before leaping onto Mandubratius' shoulder. The cat wrapped itself around his neck and continued to purr. "My feet hurt," the cat whined as it nuzzled its nose against Mandubratius' ear. "You may carry me."

"Very well," Mandubratius acknowledged before rising to his feet, wondering why he obeyed the cat. He then glanced at his clothing and realized that he did not wear armor or weapons. "Where's my fighting kit?" he asked out loud, unsure whether he asked the cat or himself.

"You are not here to join the battle," the cat informed him. "Instead, you are in Éire to bear witness to what happened. You do remember this night, do you not?"

"We collected our treasure," Mandubratius answered, though he felt a hard frown line his face. "However, it was little more than a fake."

"Mmm," the cat murmured as if in thought. "Do you want to find the real one?"

"Yes."

The cat nuzzled his ear again for a moment. "You remember nothing else?"

"What else is there to recall?" Mandubratius queried his feline guide. "We left."

"Did you, now. Did you leave in victory... or in defeat?"

"We found our prize, so we left in victory," he said, though he felt his words were uncertain.

"Clearly, your recollection is flawed. However, you will soon be reacquainted with this recent history."

Mandubratius could sense the battle move closer to their location, and he feared that they might be surrounded by the enemy.

"Do not worry, for they cannot see you," the cat informed him, as if hearing his concerns.

Just then, a warrior passed through Mandubratius as if he were an apparition, and then a loud scream pierced the air.

Mandubratius jumped at the sound and felt a cold lance of fear pierce his body from head to toe.

All the warriors stopped their combat and stared in awe at a blood-drenched figure who had emitted the scream.

"You remember that sound now, do you not?" The cat grew silent for a moment before continuing, "That sound is one of your greatest fears."

Mandubratius stared at the ground. "That is Maél Muire." He then heard a response to the challenge in the distance.

"Yes, that is Maél Muire, but she's not alone in that body," the cat chortled, as if the very sight of this carnage seemed to amuse it. Its tail rubbed Mandubratius' left ear.

"What do you mean?" Mandubratius asked as he craned his neck to look at the cat.

"Shhhh," the cat whispered in a soothing tone. "You should watch this grand skirmish."

Mandubratius watched his past self dash towards Maél Muire, wielding a sword.

The young Deargh Du seemed to draw forth strength to herself before landing a single blow to the middle of his duplicate's chest.

Mandubratius witnessed his duplicate form fly through the air. His own breath caught in his throat as he recalled the pain of Maél Muire's attack.

Amata joined his other self and ordered six of their men to carry him off the field.

The cat stood from his perch and kneaded Mandubratius' shoulder for a moment before stretching. "Now do you understand?" the cat asked.

The remaining shock of seeing Maél Muire pummel his past self made Mandubratius wobble a little. A sudden burst of pain progressed across his left cheek, and he realized that the cat had scratched him. "What was that for?" he demanded, while glaring at the cat.

"You were not paying attention to me," the cat complained with a sigh in its voice.

"Well, you have my full attention, now," Mandubratius shouted at the feline as the sting began to fade.

Even now, the wound is beginning to heal.

"Do you not see, you foolish Lamia? This is what awaits you if you return to Éire to find your prize!" The cat's voice grew and became a near-growl in his mind.

As Mandubratius looked around the grove and the surrounding fields, he saw stacks and piles of the headless corpses of Lamia and Celtic blood-drinkers strewn about, but at what cost?

Clarity grew within.

The pursuit of this treasure seems so pointless. Why have I wasted so much time... and the lives of many fellow Lamia... on this goal? I could have spent those years furthering Felician's church plans. Why didn't the Lamia just kill me for this insane idea of mine? Felician had abandoned the hunt for the relic so long ago. Why did I continue with it? I can never return to Éire.

"You have learned, and now you understand," whispered the cat.

The battlefield soon grew silent, and the bodies of the dead warriors faded away with a strange, rolling mist.

"Yes, I understand," Mandubratius acknowledged before raising his hand to rub the cat's chin.

The cat purred and began rubbing its nose against Mandubratius' neck. "My work is done, then. You have an empire to rebuild." The feline stood up again, crouched, and leapt to the grass.

The warm spot on Mandubratius' shoulders soon grew cold.

The cat walked in a half-circle around Mandubratius before sitting down and staring up at him.

Mandubratius knelt to get closer to the feline form. "So, Lord of Cats, do you have a name?"

The cat smiled at him with a most human grin. "I do have a name, Awvarwy, but I am not telling it to you. When you wake, you will not remember me at all, but you will remember the lessons from this realm."

"I won't remember you?" he asked the cat.

"That is correct. You will not remember me at all, but we will meet again, and I will tell you my name, then. Now, it is time for you to wake up."

chapter four

atroclus continued staring down at Mandubratius.

If invading Éire again is the co-consul's goal, then I will kill him. Now, how should I go about doing him in?

At that moment, Mandubratius' eyes fluttered open, and his gaze focused on Patroclus. Clarity gleamed in those clear eyes. "Patroclus," Mandubratius called to him, with a genuine smile upon his face. "It's so good to see you."

The legate tried to push away his guilt at contemplating the righteous regicide of Mandubratius, lest the elder Lamia sense it. "How is it that you are well?" he asked the co-consul.

"I don't have an answer for that now," Mandubratius replied. His eyes soon reflected an almost imperceptible growing suspicion, yet it remained veiled behind his unusual joviality. "You were thinking about killing me, were you not?"

Patroclus bit his tongue and inhaled, deciding to reveal the truth. "Only if it were necessary for the good of the Lamia, co-consul," he admitted. He backed a step away as Mandubratius, who continued smiling, sat up. Patroclus pondered Mandubratius' condition, wondering whether he was cured or remained mad.

What will he do?

Patroclus laughed inwardly, considering that this musing might be his last.

"I revise my statement," Mandubratius interjected. "You had decided to kill me... I could tell by your reaction when I awoke."

Patroclus nodded his head, wanting to avoid giving voice to the truth.

"And why did you take no action based on this decision, legate?" Mandubratius queried as he studied him. "I am still alive." He then stood up and looked down at himself. "At least, I believe I am alive."

Patroclus nodded and soon found words. "You are still alive because you have not yet given cause for me to kill you, co-consul."

"Yet? You anticipate I will give you cause?" Mandubratius examined his fingernails as he spoke.

"Perhaps," Patroclus replied. "Amata and I both believe you will soon give us cause to execute you."

Mandubratius' smile grew again. "Oh, Patroclus." He shook his head, turned, and walked over to the chair Amata frequently occupied, before sitting down. "What heinous decision do you and the lovely Amata feel I will make that would give you justification to do away with me?"

This man before me now seems very much like the Mandubratius of the past.

Patroclus held his breath and then calmed his nerves with an exhale. "Amata and I both fear you would want us to return to Éire to take the prize from the Deargh Du."

Mandubratius raised his brows.

Patroclus believed this meant Mandubratius wanted to give him time to explain himself. Part of living and working with Mandubratius in the past involved interpreting the multitude of facial expressions from the Briton. Patroclus believed few others knew the true meanings behind the co-consul's facial expressions.

"The army was devastated after the defeat," he explained to Mandubratius. Patroclus began to pace as he continued speaking. "We felt if you announced to the senate that we were to return to Hibernia, civil war would break out." The legate stopped pacing and looked at Mandubratius, gauging him for his reaction. Then the co-consul sucked on his upper lip and rubbed his bearded chin. He held back his desire to say that the campaign had been an utter failure.

Mandubratius surprised him with an admission. "I think this business with the Phallus Maximus should have been left alone." He scowled for a moment. "It was folly, sheer folly. Felician warned me about going after the prize. That bastard was right."

A wave of relief washed over Patroclus.

Eureka! The co-consul had indeed regained his senses!

"I will not repeat that error, Patroclus. Returning to Éire to find the Phallus Maximus would be insanity."

"You have been insane for over a year," Patroclus blurted out.

Mandubratius grew silent for a few seconds before speaking again. "Has it really been a year?" he muttered, before rubbing his chin again. "Yes, I remember not having a beard, then."

"We have trimmed it, from time to time," Patroclus explained.

Mandubratius extended his left hand. "There's a bronze mirror on my desk, Patroclus. Could you please hand it to me?"

Patroclus turned to his left and then found the mirror. He then handed it to the co-consul.

Mandubratius stared at himself for a moment. "I like it," he said as he set down the mirror. "Where's Amata? I'm sure she'd be delighted to hear that I have new goals for our line."

"She's in the senate chambers, now, trying to convince the senate not to elect new leadership."

Mandubratius rose from the chair. "Well, perhaps I'm needed in senate chambers. Guard!"

A praetorian opened the door, and, as he leaned in, his jaw dropped.

"Have the servants bring my clothing for me," ordered the co-consul. "Please let the senate know... never mind. I will surprise them."

The guard saluted him, shouted, "Ave co-consul," and left the room.

Mandubratius turned away from the door and examined the legate with a critical eye. "Patroclus, Patroclus. You just admitted that you and Amata were conspiring to kill me."

A chill ran up and down Patroclus' spine as he noticed that the merriment had left Mandubratius' eyes.

"However, I think your decision was not made for selfish reasons. You and Amata both believed that if I made the decision to return to Éire, the Lamia would have suffered. Therefore, I won't punish you or her, though I can say that I'm within my rights to have you executed."

Patroclus held back words and instead nodded his head.

"Good." Mandubratius turned away. "Well, you best dress for the senate. You'll be accompanying me."

Patroclus found his voice again. "Thank you for sparing me, Mandubratius."

"Now, if you don't stop dawdling, you won't be ready, and then I will execute you myself." A good-humored light grew in the co-consul's green eyes.

"Yes, co-consul, I'm going." As Patroclus left the room, he realized his face bore a mirthful grin, for Mandubratius appeared to be fully recovered.

Amata failed to restrain the exasperation projecting from her scowl as she argued her case for the recommendations she proposed.

Who wouldn't find a modicum of frustration with the male senators, who all speak in hushed voices during my discourse. They will soon start squabbling for rights to leadership, once I finish speaking.

The few female senators in the chamber remained quiet and stoic. They were new additions to the Lamia government, though few of the men would listen to their suggestions or ideas.

Why should I worry about leadership, when I might have to run for my life tonight? Of course, Patroclus will help me flee with Mandubratius, at least I hope he will.

She stopped speaking and then sat down.

The rumblings of the male senators raised in volume, as if they all were sitting together in a forica relieving them themselves of their shits after consuming too much tracta et fabam vitellianam.

Glabius, one of the male senators, rose to his feet, about to issue a motion.

As soon as his mouth opened, a clear voice bellowed from the other side of the senate chamber.

"I demand the floor!"

Amata turned her head and watched Mandubratius walk towards her, with Patroclus in tow behind him. They were both dressed in their best togas and wore weapons.

She inhaled, wondering what he would say to the rest of the Lamia gathered.

Patroclus stood behind her seat, while Mandubratius stood before his.

"My friends, I understand that some of you believe I am not fit to share leadership with our co-consul, Amata," Mandubratius intoned.

Grumbling rumbled through the marbled hall.

More flatulence of the mouth.

"I am here to cast these doubts aside, for I am here. I wish to present a new plan for our future." Mandubratius turned around and sat down next to her.

Amata experienced a moment of doubt and anxiety, fearful that he would start speaking about Hibernia, again.

Mandubratius grinned at her for a moment, revealing the confident smile she remembered from before.

Amata shifted her gaze to the senate seats and witnessed a muted Glabius returning to his seat.

Hopefully, Mandubratius will not give you cause to interrupt him.

"My friends, the Phallus Maximus is long gone. It would be madness to attempt to find it, and I am not mad. Instead, we are going to rededicate ourselves to expanding the Christian Church established here. Our church will influence all in the region, and our wealth will expand once again."

A cautious burst of applause erupted in the senate chambers.

Amata closed her eyes as her apprehension faded.

The senators began to ask questions about the renewed plans for dominating the Christian church, and Mandubratius rewarded them with poise and confidence.

It seems we may yet live another night.

epilogue

Amata pulled Mandubratius aside, as the senators finished filing out of the room. She had a feeling that their powers would diminish again with his renewed influence.

"I understand that you took care of me during my convalescence," he stated.

"It was my duty and my pleasure," she offered, unsure whether she stood in some wonderful dream.

Mandubratius' eyes turned downcast, and his face grew serious. He took her hands and whispered, "It must have been very difficult for you to be there during my illness."

"Patroclus was most helpful."

He nodded. "I know. We should consider promoting him."

Amata uttered a snort. "He hates high positions of leadership. We should give him something else instead." She stared deeply into Mandubratius' green eyes. "After all of the doctors' failures, how is it that you have recovered?"

"A miracle," he answered. His eyes revealed playfulness again. "No, it was…" He seemed to search for words. "I experienced a curious dream, and Felician was there. He said something while we were in Constantinople."

"What did he say in this dream?" she demanded.

Mandubratius' eyes turned inward, before refocusing on her. "Felician said I would never amount to anything, and he said that I would never accomplish more than he had achieved in his long life."

She nodded, knowing that Felician never saw the genius or determination in Mandubratius, not even his charms.

"I can understand how that might motivate you. The scale is tipped heavily in his favor," she reasoned aloud.

He began walking with her again through the marbled halls and out into the incense-filled corridors.

Rome awaited them.

"I can still add weight to my side," Mandubratius boasted as he smiled once again. "He cannot."

She wrapped her arm around him. "You know I will support you in tipping the scale."

"I am certain that I can do little without you, Amata."

Reckoning

a story of the
morrigan's Brood series

By

heather poinsett Dunbar
& christopher Dunbar

Reckoning occurs after the events of <u>Crone of War</u>:
Morrigan's Brood Book II and before <u>Dark Alliance</u>:
Morrigan's Brood Book III. The story takes place
during 565 CE in what is now Northern Ireland,
Wales, and England.

prologue

Outside of Óghmaigh, Éire - 565 CE

arcus Galerius Primus Helvetticus, ex-praetor of Gaul, ex-general of the seventh legion, liberator of the Deargh Du, son-in-darkness of the Phantom Queen, now relegated to cutthroat.

Marcus grumbled as he carried his burden through the woods. Every once in awhile, the man he carried moaned. A swift punch would generally silence the noise, for a short time.

He started running again, hoping his instincts were correct. He believed his supplies would be a mile to the west. The mist cooled Marcus as he ambled around the slick patches of mud dotting the green grasses of Éire. While the sickled moon lit some of his way, his enhanced vision, thanks be to Morrigan, compensated for the reduced illumination. As Marcus trudged through the brush, he listened as animals and plants whispered to the darkness, but he regretted that he could not stop to bask in their song.

After several more steps, Marcus halted his run and began to sniff the air, hoping to find his supply bag. He located it to the north. His eyes confirmed what his other senses had detected, as he spotted the gnarled, ivy covered oak, which marked the location of his bag, in the distance.

Before planning his abduction of this particular Deargh Du, he had mapped out what he believed to be a safe distance from Jarlath's home. If his target decided to run, Marcus could catch up to him and slay him as a coward.

Marcus contemplated dropping his burden on the bare ground, but he decided instead to set the leather sack and its contents on the grass with care. He removed his pouch of blood mead and took a long draw from it. After quenching his thirst, he reattached it to his belt and then began to gather the tools he needed for this undesirable task.

Once prepared, Marcus knelt next to the sack containing the unconscious Jarlath and started to undo the laces. Soon, the bound and gagged victim appeared from within the confines of the brown, leather sack.

Marcus picked up a bucket of water from behind the rest of the supplies he had set aside previously and dumped it on Jarlath's face.

The other Deargh Du awoke, sputtering through the gag.

"Jarlath," Marcus called as he pulled on the other man's tunic, helping him to sit up. "I suppose you're wondering why you're here in the middle of the woods." He untied the gag and backed away, expecting the other blood-drinker to break through the rope bindings. Marcus did not have to wait long.

"How dare you kidnap me?" the Deargh Du demanded as he stood, tossing aside the now rent ropes. "What gives you the right to take me from my home?"

Marcus shrugged a bit. "You've been a thorn in Sáerlaith's side, and so she wishes for me to take care of this matter in a permanent manner."

Jarlath's face turned a strange shade of gray. "Sáerlaith put you up to this? When I get back to Ard Mhacha, I'll make sure everyone knows of this atrocity!"

Marcus cocked an eye at Jarlath, wondering whether his Gaelic had failed him, or perhaps the other Deargh Du just ignored plain-speaking explanations.

"When you return to Ard Mhacha?" he asked.

Jarlath stared back him. "You and Sáerlaith mean to bring me there as leverage against my friends and associates. I will be asked to make concessions, and then I will be released."

"You expect to be released after your threats to those who hold a different point of view?" Marcus asked. He walked around Jarlath, knelt, and then picked up one of the two swords positioned behind the other Deargh Du. "I'm not your kidnapper, Jarlath. I am your executioner."

Jarlath turned his head to glare at Marcus. Jarlath's gray skin seemed paler. "What? Why do this, take me from my home, just to kill me? You could have killed me during my hunt."

"It would not have been sporting, as you were unarmed," Marcus answered as he stood, holding the gladius, and then walked to his original spot.

Jarlath's eyes followed his every step.

"Sporting?" Jarlath challenged, outrage evident in his tone. He took a step closer to Marcus, and Marcus witnessed Jarlath's eyes turn a gleaming green. "I'm no animal or mortal to be hunted!"

"This is why I offer the option of single combat," Marcus answered. "If you defeat me, you will be free to go. If you fail to be victorious, you will be dead."

"And if I run?" Jarlath asked.

"Then you have the same chance as any other hunted beast, but your cowardice would be known amongst all Deargh Du. You would lose your political standing, assuming you managed to escape."

Jarlath seemed to consider those options for a moment. "I don't suppose there is anything I can give you to persuade you not to kill me?"

"Sadly, no," Marcus replied. "I am duty bound as one of the Cothromaigh to take your life, though frankly I couldn't care less whether you lived or died. Behind you is a gladius. I know it is shorter than what you're used to, but I didn't want to strain myself carrying more weapons and supplies than usual."

Jarlath turned to regard the sword and then returned his gaze to Marcus. "Even with that sword, do I have any chance of besting you?" Jarlath asked.

Though he hid it well, Marcus could see fear behind the other Deargh Du's green, glowing eyes.

Marcus considered the question and tried to think of an appropriate answer. "I only have one sword, so that puts me at a disadvantage, because I prefer two."

"Yes," the other Deargh Du grunted. "However, I haven't wielded a sword in centuries."

Marcus uttered a laugh before covering his mouth. "You haven't wielded a sword in that long, and yet you threatened to take out all of the Council of Five?"

"No..." Jarlath rumbled. "I would have had others perform the execution." He paused a moment, as if considering a discussion point in a debate. "Is it not dishonorable to challenge one with lower skills?"

"I am your executioner," Marcus replied. "That doesn't mean it needs to be a balanced battle. Now, are you going to pick up that sword, or will you flee like a cowardly beast?" Marcus backed away, giving the other Deargh Du more space to consider his next move.

Jarlath turned towards the sword, squatted to pick it up, and then, just before touching the pommel, Marcus saw the other Deargh Du tense and knew instantly that Jarlath planned to run. He prepared himself.

At that moment, Jarlath launched into the air.

Marcus sighed in disgust, and then threw his gladius before Jarlath could fly too far. The blade plunged into Jarlath's back below his shoulders.

The other blood-drinker fell to the ground, slamming into many tree branches on the way down, tearing cloth and skin.

Marcus picked up his other gladius, the one he had offered to Jarlath, and wiped off the dirt on his brocs. He then approached the other Deargh Du, who lay upon his belly, and watched him flail as he attempt to pull the sword from his back. "I am disappointed with you."

Jarlath uttered a gurgle. "This is not over," he growled, before coughing up blood. "My friends will avenge me."

Marcus knelt onto Jarlath's left shoulder, eliciting more pain. He allowed Jarlath to see the blade before grabbing the other Deargh Du's hair. Marcus pulled Jarlath's head up and stared into his angry eyes.

"Your allies are already dead," he announced, before severing Jarlath's head from his neck.

Only the animals, the grass, and trees whispered a response.

Blood spurted from the grievous wound, but soon, only a trickle dribbled into the bloody sod from Jarlath's headless corpse.

Marcus dropped Jarlath's head to the dirt and stared at it, before kicking at it with his toe.

"I never understood why someone would want to keep the head," Marcus quipped to the blood-soaked grass.

chapter one

Ard Mhacha, Éire

The very moment Marcus walked into their rooms, Máire voiced two questions. "What took you so long? Why are you covered in blood?" She glared at him with her luxurious, emerald-green eyes.

He had managed to ignore the whispers of 'who was it this time?' and 'who will die next' as he strolled through the stronghold, yet ignoring her sharp tongue proved something else altogether.

Máire sat in the large tub. Her long hair, the color of dried blood, lay unrestrained over her shoulders. Her hair always reminded him of Morrigan's.

A servant walked past him and dumped a large cauldron of hot water into the half-full tub.

Marcus watched Máire hold her tongue, regarding the heat of the water, but he could read annoyance in her eyes. He began undressing. Once he removed his belt and gladii, he handed them to the woman holding the empty cauldron.

He then passed the rest of his clothing to another servant. "Please clean these if possible, Brigid."

Both mortals left, their eyes downcast.

"I was outside of Óghmaigh, fulfilling Sáerlaith's wishes," he whispered in answer to her earlier questions. He then heard a snort and glanced at Máire.

"What did you do, butcher him?" she asked.

Marcus walked over to the smaller basin on the wooden table and began washing himself, deciding to ignore the fact that the tub could hold two. He started washing his hands and fingers. "I gave Jarlath a fighting chance." He glanced over at Máire, who stared back at him with shock in her eyes.

"You didn't just kill him in his sleep?"

"I'm not an assassin, Máire." He found such acts to be barbaric, the last resort of cowards.

"So, let me make sure I understand you." Máire leaned forward, grabbed a handful of lavender near the tub, and then tossed it in. "You did not kill Jarlath in his home?"

"Correct."

"So you took Jarlath from his home, unconscious?"

Marcus looked back to Máire, who stretched out her legs and then propped her feet on the opposite edge of the bath.

"Yes–"

"You dragged him to someplace in the woods," she challenged, interrupting Marcus, "and then you woke him, gave him one of your gladii, and told him to fight you?"

"Something like that, but–"

"Tell me, Marcus," she growled, interrupting him again. "What level of skill was he with a blade? Was Jarlath a warrior?"

"You know him, he isn't a–"

Máire cut him off again. "Then tell me, General Marcus Galerius Primus Helvetticus, former Praetor of Gaul, leader of the Celtic lines against the Lamia invaders, how skillful at warfare are you?"

Marcus stared at the floor, knowing very well what Máire meant.

"There is no way you could have fought Jarlath on an equal footing. Claudius once told me that it is dishonorable for a Roman soldier to challenge one as weak as Jarlath. His death was an assassination, and you are an assassin, as I am."

He felt stung by her conclusion.

"Your water is cooling, and you still smell of blood." Máire commented while staring at his forgotten basin. He picked up a cloth, dunked it in the water, and started washing himself again, deciding to say nothing further.

He soon heard the sounds of splashing again from the bath.

"Did you not believe Jarlath needed to die?" Máire asked.

Marcus regarded Máire for a moment, but he decided to pretend that the earlier silence remained unbroken.

"I'm surprised, with all the people you have killed, that this one death brings you such discomfort," Máire scoffed.

He threw the towel into the basin in anger and frustration. "It is not this one death!" he roared, before realizing that he had just answered her question. He then swallowed his rage and returned to a whisper. "There are always ears in this place." He turned away from the table and walked towards the tub. Once at its edge, Marcus knelt down and stared at Máire. "It's all these murders we've been asked to carry out," he continued in a hushed voice, "all for the sake of politics."

Máire shook her head. "No, they were all in the name of the Balance, and these will not be the last deaths."

Marcus leaned closer to Máire. "I find much discomfort with this mission, killing people who are not warriors in such a cowardly manner, while they slumber, and yet you seem to have no difficulty assassinating people."

"That is correct, I have no difficulty," she admitted. "The way I kill them, no. I stay in their room, hiding behind my veil of darkness. After they go to sleep, I use glamoury to set them at peace, and then I behead them." Máire shrugged before sitting up and drifting closer to him. "They have pleasant thoughts on their way home."

She paused before looking at his face. Then she raised a finger to his left brow and scratched. She pulled back her finger and revealed to him the flakes of dried blood she had scraped from his face. "I don't get myself covered in their blood," she chided as she retracted her arm and leaned back.

Marcus reached his left arm towards her withdrawing form, but instead of grabbing her wrist, he settled for tracing a finger over her damp right arm. "Máire, it pains me to hear you speak of this, as if you enjoy murdering people in their sleep."

She let out a resigned sigh. "I take no pleasure in it, Marcus. I just carry it out. That is all. Now, are you going to share the tub with me, or shall I leave you to the bowl?"

As she stared at him with her brazen eyes, Marcus realized that this was not the same woman who asked him to be her father-in-darkness. Since Seosaimhín had cursed Máire, she felt like a stranger who shared his blood. He looked back at the table and the basin, considering whether to join Máire in the bath or avoid her company, when he heard a splash from the tub and felt cool drops of water strike his bare back. Marcus turned to regard his daughter-in-darkness.

Máire rose from the tub and leaned over to pick up a drying cloth from the opposite side of the bath. She stepped out of the tub and began to dry herself. "I'll take this to mean that you wish to be alone." She paused before turning to look him over. "Pity…" Her words rang with distaste. "Come to my bed, when you've found your balls."

Sáerlaith's body passed through the mist, and then sunlight embraced her with warmth, causing her elation to triple. She closed and opened her eyes, before witnessing a figure, whom she recognized as Morrigan, seated on a stone in the distance. Sáerlaith approached Her slowly, entranced by the spraying waterfall that cooled her, and then knelt before her race's progenitor.

"No need to kneel, My child. Sit next to Me," the Crone Goddess bade, before patting the stone seat next to Her.

Sáerlaith stood, took a few steps, and sat down. She felt awestruck that Morrigan would give her such a high honor. "Thank you, Grandmother."

"What force brings your shoulders so low?" Morrigan asked in a voice that poured musically from the air, the land, the trees, and Her mouth. Morrigan rested Her hand on Sáerlaith's knee.

Sáerlaith turned her head towards the One-Eyed Crone, but she felt she could not make eye contact with Her. "I'm troubled by my actions of late," she said to the

Goddess.

"*I can understand,*" Morrigan began to explain. "*Every action has consequences, and many times they will be unexpected. You are worried about the deaths that you, Marcus, and Máire have instigated.*" Morrigan's tone was that of a concerned grandmother, desiring, without judgment, to help.

"*Yes, Grandmother. I've taken the lives of those who voiced their desire to remain isolationists. I fear that for each silenced voice, many more will be swayed to that ideal.*"

Morrigan stood up and stepped over Sáerlaith's feet.

Sáerlaith tried to rise, but the Goddess put out Her left hand to keep Sáerlaith seated.

Morrigan squatted in front of her and placed Her hands on Sáerlaith's knees.

Sáerlaith remembered her mother, on many occasions when she had been a mortal youth, kneeling so that they could speak at eye-level. She fell into the depths of Morrigan's eye as it reflected a strength and deep love.

"*Do what you must, Sáerlaith. This is your decision. However, remember that whatever you decide will bring about consequences. You must choose,*" the Goddess intoned.

Sáerlaith felt some assurance from Morrigan's declaration. "*Thank you, Grandmother,*" she said, feeling lost within the Goddess' love.

Morrigan smiled and then rose with an unearthly grace that left Sáerlaith breathless. The Goddess leaned in to kiss Sáerlaith's brow.

Sáerlaith closed her eyes at the blissful and otherworldly touch. She opened her eyes, only to gaze upon candlelight. A familiar chin, which did not belong to the Goddess, disrupted her thoughts and obstructed the glow from the flame.

Soon the chin pulled away, and the dreamy state of the Otherworld disappeared.

Sáerlaith felt a sudden outburst of frustration as her connection with the other realm withered like a dying oak leaf. She slapped Marcus across the face, causing the other Deargh Du to step back, holding his cheek. "Never interrupt me when I'm walking the mists!" Sáerlaith yelled, angry over the intrusion.

Marcus' eyes shifted to gazing at the floor in what seemed like embarrassment. "I apologize. I'll leave." His stuttered response released Sáerlaith from her anger, leaving her enfolded in guilt and a little annoyance.

She grabbed his left arm and bade, "Sit down, please," but Marcus hesitated. She looked up at him and exclaimed, "Sit, or I will hit you again!"

Marcus now resembled a sad-eyed dog or a scolded child.

Sáerlaith released his arm and then patted the bed next to her.

He sat down beside her.

"Why are you here at such an early hour? You should be sleeping." She studied him again, now feeling a little spellbound by his beauty. "Did you kill Jarlath, as I had asked?"

He looked at her, and his eyes revealed aching sorrow. "Yes, I assassinated Jarlath in cold blood, as he was running away from me."

That answer confused her. "You did not kill him in his sleep?"

His back became straight and his eyes now reflected growing fury. "I..." His frown grew deeper. "I just had this conversation with Máire, and I won't have it again!" Marcus placed his hands on the bed and pushed himself up.

Sáerlaith grasped his wrist and stared at him, allowing her glamoury to surround him.

Marcus calmed and then nodded in supplication.

Sáerlaith cleared her throat, willing herself to sound congenial. "What troubles you, Marcus? Tell me about this conversation you had with Máire."

Marcus regarded her as he said, "My father died at the hands of an assassin, Sáerlaith. I've hated them all my life, and now I am one."

She felt her curiosity grow. Sáerlaith decided to allow him to lead the conversation.

Marcus stared at her and said nothing more.

Perhaps there were greater undercurrents in his mood.

"Are you telling me that you hate yourself?" she queried, not wanting the silence to last any longer.

Marcus' eyes shifted to the bed and blankets. "I like to kill when my enemy has an equal chance of killing me. That is an honorable fight. Much of my upbringing as a Roman and as a Deargh Du is based on honor." His eyes then shifted to hers. "In fact, I believed that we pursued honorable means to achieve justified ends. I have challenged each of my victims to single combat. I have given each of them one of my weapons with the belief that this meant they had an equal chance to slay me, but Máire..." Marcus said in a grave tone before pausing.

He scratched his chin and then continued. "Máire showed me that these politicians and Druids whom I killed were far beneath my skill and that their deaths at my hands were without honor."

Sáerlaith bit her tongue, having heard many of her own concerns expressed by him without her having to ask further questions. She reached up with both hands and with gentle force turned Marcus' head so he could face her. Sáerlaith stared into his gray eyes, seeking a connection with him.

"I understand," Sáerlaith whispered. "I will not ask that of you again."

Instead, I will ask Máire, who has no qualms killing those who slight her and her father-in-darkness.

Sáerlaith knew for a fact that there were several who Máire would enjoy killing.

She looked at Marcus and witnessed gratitude in his eyes, yet some worry still remained. He appeared very young, now.

Sáerlaith smiled as she gripped his hands. She then pushed Marcus onto the bed and straddled him.

"Don't worry, a stóirín. I will take care of everything," she whispered before leaning down to kiss Marcus.

Máire woke up from a dreamless sleep and realized she was not alone in the bed.

Marcus probably decided to join me.

She rolled over and began patting the blankets, hoping to wake him so she could chide him about waiting for her to fall asleep before. After opening her eyes, she blinked as she tried to identify the figure lying next to her.

That's not Marcus.

Máire rubbed her eyes as the figure rolled over, and she saw that it was Sáerlaith who lay next to her, blinking her own eyes.

"Sáerlaith?"

The other female yawned into her hand. "Máire, I hope you slept well," Sáerlaith mumbled as she sat up.

"I thought you were Marcus," Máire stated, feeling a little surprised.

"Well, I'm not Marcus." Sáerlaith cleared her throat. "He did come visit me earlier this morning, after you castrated him, or at least that's the tale he spins. He seems to want to be mothered, right now. Anyway, he tossed, turned, and grumbled about you in his sleep. So, I figured there would be an empty half of your bed available. Besides, I'm exhausted." Sáerlaith slid back under the covers.

"Yes, he is a restless sleeper, these days," Máire admitted, though she didn't want to say more about why Marcus couldn't find sleep.

Sáerlaith turned towards Máire. "You will be pleased to hear that I have relieved Marcus of his duties."

Máire sat up. "Does this mean there will be no more killings?"

Sáerlaith's brown eyes began to turn green. "Actually, I had been hoping that you would complete his work, Máire."

"Who would you like me to kill?"

"Two names come to mind, but before I give you those names, I must think on this for awhile. Let me sleep on it." Sáerlaith closed her eyes and pulled the blanket up to her chin.

Máire curled up and joined Sáerlaith in slumber.

chapter two

The sun warmed him as he stretched his arms over his head. He viewed the beach in front of him and looked on as men, women, and children cavorted in the warm, blue waves under the midday sun, taking a break from their holiday villas at Herculaneum.

"Wine." Marcus extended an arm and then felt the weight of a cup in his right hand. He could hear a slave open a jug, and soon the scent of honey wine mixed with the salty air. Then he felt and heard a fan begin waving over him. Marcus sipped at his wine, savoring the shade and the other comforts around him.

After finishing his wine, Marcus extended his arm again, and another slave took the goblet.

Marcus relaxed and closed his eyes, comforted by the rhythmic movements of the fan and the soothing sounds of the waves as they rolled to the shore. He could still see the fan's shadow move across his face through his closed lids.

After a few minutes of blissful relaxation, the fan stopped its rhythmic movement yet his face remained covered in shade. Soon after, all sound ceased. The noise from the other beachgoers and the ocean faded into silence.

He sat up and opened his eyes.

Instead of a sun-filled sky replete with clouds and birds, only darkness greeted him. The nighttime skies seemed to be bereft of stars, and the darkness felt overwhelming. No children frolicked in the calm surf. No slaves waited by his side. No animals greeted the night.

Marcus sat up and placed his feet on the sand. He felt a strange dread.

Did everyone leave me behind?

"Hello?" he called out, but no one answered. He gasped for breath and woke up.

Marcus rolled onto his side to wrap an arm around Sáerlaith to reassure himself that he was not alone, but his arm could not find her. He patted the covers and then opened his eyes, seeing no sign of her.

"Sáerlaith?" He sat up and scooted towards the edge of the bed to view the rest of her room.

Lovely. I've been abandoned, again.

Marcus stood up and began to look for his clothes.

At least Sáerlaith displays passion during coitus, unlike some women who possess the emotional warmth of a cold fish… Damn it all, I've got a fucking erection growing.

He considered taking care of the matter himself, but his desire for Sáerlaith's comfort won out. He found his robe on the floor and threw it on.

He walked to the door leading to the hall and opened it. Marcus concentrated on his senses and found her in his quarters, or at least the quarters he shared with Máire. Marcus walked down the hall with as much silence as he could muster. When he arrived at his door, he opened it tiptoed into the room. He felt confusion upon realizing both Sáerlaith and Máire shared their bed. He caught himself smiling and forgot his earlier hurt.

Sáerlaith slept on her side with her back to the wall, while Máire lay with her body turned away from him.

Marcus dropped his robe, pulled up the covers, and positioned himself in bed on his side, behind her. Several times before he had awaken Máire in such a manner, and each time she had rewarded him for his resourcefulness and creativity.

He slid Máire's léine up her side until he could slide his right hand over her right breast. He tweaked her nipple, before moving his hand down her body so he could caress her loins. As he gently stroked her petals, she became wet and began to moan.

Marcus gripped her waist and scooted his hips closer to her. When he was close enough, he lifted her cheek and started to penetrate her.

With a moan, Máire stirred, and the motion made him forget his earlier complaints about her cool detachment.

Máire stiffened and seemed to wake completely. "Sáerlaith?" she muttered.

Marcus tensed, now unsure how Máire will react to his intimate embrace.

"What?" the other woman grumbled in sleep.

Máire turned her head, opened her eyes, and regarded him. "Marcus?" Embarrassment and astonishment shone in her eyes. She elbowed him hard in his chest, knocking him out of the bed.

He felt some shock as he landed onto the cold, stone floor.

"Marcus, we have company." Máire covered her exposed skin with her léine and then tried to smooth down her unkempt hair.

Sáerlaith sat up and looked confused. "What's going on?" She scooted out of the bed and stared down at Marcus, sans his erection. "Oh, I see."

"I apologize," Máire stated while pushing her hair behind her ears. "He surprised me... oh by the Gods." She turned pink, before sliding under the covers. "I'm so embarrassed."

"Since..." Sáerlaith seemed to look for words. "I... I will leave you both alone. You obviously need to talk." She fixed her gaze at Marcus. "I'm sorry, a stóirín. If Máire leaves any piece of you intact, come visit me, later." Sáerlaith then walked around him to Máire's side of the bed and pulled back the cover. She kissed Máire's brow, whispered something to her, and then left the room.

Marcus remained on the floor, unsure of what to say to Máire.

Perhaps I should just leave and follow Sáerlaith.

"Are you still on the floor?"

He noticed Máire staring at him from the bed, though most of her remained covered in blankets. She threw back the covers, looking quite enraged. "Get your flaccid cock off the floor and in this bed." Máire reclined again and pulled the blankets over her head.

He sighed before getting to his feet. Marcus stepped over to the opposite side of the bed and slid under the covers.

Máire rolled onto her side, away from him.

His desire for intimacy swelled within him again, and so Marcus scooted closer to Máire and placed a hand on her backside.

"I did not move into this position for you to enter me, so don't think on it."

"Then w–"

Máire cut him off. "Sáerlaith has tasked me with killing two more people."

All of Marcus' amorous thoughts left him. "I thought this was done," he pronounced.

"No. She's not going to ask you to kill anyone, because you can't handle the job," Máire replied.

"By Juno's cunt!" he exclaimed. "She lied to me!"

Máire uncovered her head and rolled over to face him. "Did Sáerlaith not tell you that you didn't have to murder anyone else?"

He grew silent, mulling over the answer to that question. "Yes, but–"

"There, you see? The truth is as bright as the sun," Máire growled with sarcasm, before her voice grew silent.

He felt reluctance at admitting to the fact. "You're correct," he whispered. "Yet, how could you agree to murder more Deargh Du?"

"Because that is my duty," Máire answered.

Marcus felt the sting in her words.

Máire rolled away from him and then began to adjust the covers. After a few moments, she stopped shifting the blankets. "You may enter, now," Máire informed him.

Marcus felt a growing puzzlement at her statement. Uncertainty prevented him from considering what to do next. His earlier amorousness seemed to be a distant memory.

Máire snuck into the room of her next victim and looked for the most shadowy corner near the ceiling. After finding it, she wrapped herself in darkness and then levitated to the inky corner. She held her breath and willed her heart to stop. Marcus had taught her well how to hide and become one with the shadows. He had also demonstrated how to adjust the gloom so that one could peer out from it and still be concealed.

Soon, the door opened and shut.

Máire peeked through the edge of the darkness she created and watched her target, Aisling, and a mortal servant enter the room. The servant placed warm water in the washbasin.

"Do you wish for a bath, my lady?"

Aisling stepped out of her léine and passed the dirty garment to the servant, before washing her hands and face.

"No. I believe I'm too sleepy, Cessair. Go back to your family and sleep well."

The servant girl and the Deargh Du kissed, and then the servant left the room.

Aisling climbed into her bed and closed her eyes. After a few minutes, the Deargh Du rolled onto her side.

Máire listened to Aisling's breathing grow long and deep. Máire mused for a moment on how strange it seemed that Deargh Du, including herself, still felt the desire to breathe, even though breathing was unnecessary. She closed her eyes and began concentrating on the activities outside of Aisling's home. Soon, the sun would rise. Already, she could sense the people of the village and their animals begin to wake.

After waiting for almost two hours, Máire reached out with her glamoury and suggested to Aisling that she enjoy her beautiful dreams and ignore anything in the world of the waking that might disturb her. Máire began to descend from the ceiling but kept the gloom around her. Two feet above the other Deargh Du, Máire drew her short sword from her belt and prepared to behead Aisling. With a two-handed grip, she raised her sword and began to swing it towards her target. However, an unexpected voice caused Máire to abort her strike.

"Get out of my head! It's very rude to use your glamoury on another Deargh Du."

Máire gasped and then shut her mouth, before retracting her glamoury.

"You are the worst at concealing yourself. I sensed you the very moment I walked into my home," Aisling added.

Máire released the darkness surrounding her before floating up towards the ceiling. She continued to hold her sword at the ready in case she needed to defend herself.

"I wondered when you would pay me a visit, since one by one, you and Marcus have eliminated my friends," Aisling alleged.

Máire said nothing but wondered why she could not force herself now to kill Aisling.

"What is wrong, youngling? You can't murder someone who is awake? Rós told me how Marcus gave his victims the opportunity to defend themselves. Though, I believe, he was simply trying to find some amusement in watching pitiful men and women, who had gone for so long without wielding a sword, die at the hands of Rome's finest champion," Aisling mocked. "At least your bastard father-in-darkness lets his victims die on their feet. Yours all die in their sleep. I refuse to die in my bed, so if you want to kill me, at least allow me to rise and die with some dignity!"

"Do... do you wish to fight me?" Máire stuttered. She felt her face begin to burn.

Aisling uttered a cackling laugh. "I am no warrior, you spawn of that Roman atrocity. You would defeat me so easily. Regardless of my skill level, I refuse to lower myself to fighting you."

Again, Máire found no words.

Aisling stared into Máire's eyes with a piercing glare. "I'm speaking to you! Have you not heard a word I've uttered? Are you going to allow me to leave my bed?"

"Yes." Máire lowered herself to the ground a few feet away from Aisling, though she continued to grip her sword with both hands, preparing to defend herself.

Aisling stretched before sitting up in her bed. She popped her neck to the side and then turned her body towards Máire.

"Why are you naked?" she asked Máire.

Máire squeaked a bit. "This makes it easier to wash up before I go home."

The blonde woman's mouth twitched a bit in a strange revelation of amusement. "I suppose that makes sense. Alright, I'm ready. Dispatch me. No, wait. I should undress.. that way you can make certain I have no weapons." Aisling crossed her arms over her chest.

"That is not necessary," Máire informed Aisling.

The other woman lowered her arms, letting her léine fall back into place. Aisling nodded her golden head. "Fine, then. Kill me."

Máire sought her resolve from her earlier attempt to eliminate her target. After taking a deep but useless, breath, Máire's determination returned, and she lifted her blade, preparing to slice off Aisling's head.

"But first, tell me why I must die," Aisling demanded.

Máire hesitated.

Why can I not simply command my muscles to work? What holds me back? Fear? No. Do I have second thoughts about killing my target? No. I have no doubts. I have my duty, and I will carry it out. Yet, I feel I need to address Aisling's simple question. Why…?

"Because I was told to kill you," Máire enunciated, hoping her voice sounded steady and assured.

Why must I justify myself to this woman?

Aisling interrupted her thoughts. "Oh, yes. You and that father-in-darkness of yours were told, like soldiers, what to do. You both are always following orders without thinking for yourselves." Aisling sighed. "You look to be Gael and you're Deargh Du, but you stink of Rome and the Lamia." After a brief pause, Aisling continued. "Let me guess… Sáerlaith is the puppet master. You needn't answer with your tongue… your expression confirms her complicity."

Máire felt like ice, as Aisling resumed her ranting.

"Do you believe that what Sáerlaith is doing is right? Do you think assassinating political opposition is best for the Deargh Du? Is it balanced?"

The last sentence echoed in Máire's mind. She felt her two-handed grip on her sword begin to weaken. As her resolve wavered, the tip of her blade lowered. There could be only one answer to Aisling's question, but Máire could not voice it. She no longer had the strength to hold her sword, and with a loud clank, the weapon struck the stone floor and became still.

"I did not think so," Aisling answered, righteous smugness and distaste dripping from her words. "I thank you for not killing me, though I do not consider your sparing me a favor. You only spared me to sate your conscience. Now, since it is daylight, you will not be able to return home. Therefore, I am making you a guest in my home. As my honored guest, I offer you my bed, that is if you promise not to kill me in my sleep."

Máire felt her face burn with shame.

I failed Sáerlaith. I failed Marcus! Adding insult to injury, my target has accepted me as her guest. How can I live with this shame?

Máire blinked away her tears. "When I depart, you will be unharmed."

"Excellent," Aisling answered, though with less smugness than before. "I also pledge to allow you to depart, unharmed. After all, were I to kill you, my honored guest, what kind of host would I be?"

Máire stepped over to the bed and offered, "I will share it with you."

"No," Aisling answered in a calm, yet focused tone. No smugness or indignation colored her voice. She smiled and said, "I shall sleep on the floor. My guests receive the best of my home." Aisling approached her. "If you require clothing, I'll call for Cessair to bring you my finest léine. If you wish to bathe, I will have her draw you a bath as well. Oh, and do you need to feed?"

"You are most kind," Máire managed to say without stammering, though her embarrassment still burned deep within her. "However, that will not be necessary," she insisted, though her own odors revealed the need for a bath, and she did need sustenance after using her gifts earlier during this encounter. Still, Máire did not wish to admit to her needs.

I have failed. Therefore, I will suffer.

"Alright then. I trust you need no assistance getting into bed." Despite her words and despite the situation, Máire found no patronizing in Aisling's tone.

"I can manage," Máire whispered, unable to hide her meekness as she pulled back the covers. She glanced towards Aisling before climbing into bed in order to thank her for her generosity. Though Máire knew this encounter would result in dire consequences tonight, Aisling had been quite civil, more so than Máire would have been had the situation been reversed.

Aisling caught Máire by surprise and embraced her, kissing her cheek. "Sleep well then."

Máire found herself returning the embrace and the kiss.

Aisling released her and walked to the other side of the room.

Máire sat on the edge of the bed, lifted her legs, and slid into the bed.

I wish to Morrigan, to Lugh Lamfada, to anyone, that the sun will magically plummet, causing the night to be borne early.

With deep desperation, Máire desired for this day of humiliation to end. Before closing her eyes, Máire looked on as the other Deargh Du prepared for bed.

Aisling grabbed furs and a few spare blankets, before placing them on the floor on the opposite side of the bed. The other Deargh Du then reclined on the floor and wrapped herself in her bedding. Aisling closed her eyes and seemed to drift off to sleep.

I could kill her, now, and snatch victory from the jaws of defeat. No one would be the wiser that Aisling had in fact defanged me with a challenge of words. No one would know about her generosity to me, her would-be assassin. No one would know about our agreement not to kill one another this day. No one would know... but me. But I gave Aisling my word that I would not kill her. Honor, and shame, demand that I respect our agreement.

So, instead of rolling out of bed, grabbing her sword, flying over to her target, and severing Aisling's head from her body, Máire pulled the covers over herself and curled up onto her left side. Soon, she sobbed herself to sleep, hoping Aisling already slept and wouldn't hear her crying.

chapter three

Marcus blew the sawdust off the figure carefully, while trying to keep the candles lit. He examined the carving, wondering whether any attempts to capture the Warrior Queen's true essence would lead to failure. He decided he would wait until he completed the rest of the carving before starting on Her face and hair.

He soon heard someone clear her throat, so he looked up to see Máire staring down at him with an unreadable expression. He inhaled, attempting to determine whether she smelled of spilled blood, but aside from her body odor, Marcus could detect no whiff of blood about her.

"What are you carving?" she asked. Máire's tone revealed little more than her features.

Marcus held up the figure in his left hand while he held his knife in his right in a relaxed grip.

Máire drew closer and beheld the object in his hand.

"It is Morrigan," he said.

"She's lovely." Máire's hand wrapped around his left hand, and then she scrutinized his work at closer range. "It looks like you're almost finished. When did you find the time to work on this?"

"I am good at carving, and expeditious," he admitted. "Besides, I have more time, now, and no other purpose to dominate my waking moments."

"But you have a purpose, Marcus," she insisted as she lowered her hand.

"Do I, Maél Muire?" He threw his hands up in anger, careful to prevent the carving and his knife from flying out of his hands. "I'm a general without an army to lead or a war to fight. I have no purpose."

"I am called Máire, now."

She can be utterly oblivious sometimes.

He threw his knife in disgust at the floor beneath them, which bit a chip out of the stone floor, yet the impact was not without consequence for the instrument. Marcus could see from his vantage point that he would need to put his whet stone to good use to sharpen out the gash in the cutting blade.

"Yes, Máire, heartless killer, heartless lover. Máire, who inhabits Maél Muire's body! Sometimes, Maél Muire, I wish I hadn't changed you. You were so vibrant, then. You were caring, then! I loved you, then!" He did not mean to say those words, as his heart did not feel this way. Yet, after what she and Sáerlaith had put him through, he cared little for holding back his anger.

She appeared to suppress tears. "Marcus, I can't help who I've become.

You and Morrigan gave me great gifts, but Seosaimhín poisoned me, poisoned me in a way that will stay with me for as long as I walk the night." His daughter-in-darkness then looked away. "Morrigan named me well, did she not? I am bitter."

He felt some surprise at her display of emotion.

Perhaps her emotional restraint is something else, something other than a curse. Oh, how I wish someone could cure her of this affliction. I miss how she used to be.

Marcus ceased his introspection and recalled sensing an absence of something on her body. "I noticed you did not smell of blood, Máire. Something is wrong. What happened?"

Máire's face fell, and then she collapsed to her knees. She placed her hands on his legs and started to cry over his lap.

Fearful of eavesdropping Deargh Du, Marcus knelt on the floor and drew himself closer to her.

Máire grabbed his shoulders and pulled herself to him.

Marcus wrapped her in an embrace and rested his left cheek against hers. "Tell me what happened," he whispered.

She started hyperventilating. "I... I... didn't kill her!" Máire began to cry. Tears flowed down her cheeks and his.

"There, there," he cooed as he stroked Máire's back. All the possible scenarios of what had happened and what could happen to them flashed in his head.

Máire seems to be calming down, yet my tunic is now wet from her tears.

"Now, tell me what happened, please," he soothed. Marcus relaxed his hold on Máire.

"I went to take care of Aisling," she began to explain.

He nodded. "I think I've heard of her."

"She was waiting for me. She knew I was there. She knew I used my glamoury."

He scanned Máire's face with his eyes. Marcus then held her at arm's length and inspected the rest of her body, concluding that she did not appear to have suffered any wounds. "So, she fought you?" he asked.

"With words. She fought me with words."

He fell silent, stunned that someone managed to talk Máire out of killing them. Marcus released Máire completely and sat back on his heels. "She talked you out of killing her? What do you mean? Did she beg for her life?" Marcus asked, unable to hide his incredulous tone.

Máire shook her head. "No. She told me that killing her would not be balanced." Her crying resumed, and she could not keep herself from hyperventilating.

Marcus remembered seeing Máire as the young mortal he had rescued from her burning house, how he had seen her as a woman, and then how she appeared after he had made her Deargh Du.

I can not be angry with her. She needs me. She needs her father-in-darkness.

"What do you believe she meant by that, Máire?" Marcus whispered, in what he hoped was a calming voice.

Máire sat back on her feet and wiped her face once more. After a few moments, she seemed to calm herself enough to talk. "Aisling demanded that I hurry and kill her after she told me it was unbalanced. I dropped my sword, and then she accepted me as her guest. She gave me her bed and slept on the floor." Máire uttered a strained noise. "Then, when the sun set, she fed me herself before I left. She shamed me, Marcus. That harmed me more than any blade could."

How Aisling managed to fight off Máire's glamoury and convince Máire not to kill her still escapes my reasoning. However, Aisling's use of local customs to shame Máire intrigues me. This woman must be a formidable adversary, worthy of respect.

Máire's green eyes met his. "I don't know what to do! Aisling knows who sent me! I have failed Sáerlaith and I have failed Morrigan. What should I do, Marcus? What should I do?" No tears came after this outburst, but Marcus could see the desperation, the fear, in her eyes.

He stared back at her, considering what they might have to do to survive this unfortunate circumstance. "There is only one thing to do. We must talk to Sáerlaith."

"But I failed–"

He raised his hand, and Máire fell silent.

"We must accept the consequences, and so must Sáerlaith." He stood up and offered Máire a hand. "Come... we have to speak to her... now." He dreaded Sáerlaith's reaction to this news. However, he found some relief that Máire had lost her taste for killing Deargh Du. Their nights of shame would end, now.

He helped Máire to her feet, and they began to walk to Sáerlaith's offices, arm in arm.

Sáerlaith felt intolerably alone within the Deargh Du stronghold of Ard Mhacha. The warriors, many of whom fought with her against the Lamia, assured her protection, but a majority of them often slept outside of the stronghold during the day. The Druids, in turn, occupied most of the residential areas of their home. The rest of the Council of Five stayed within the other kingdoms of Éire. As the chief councilor, Sáerlaith held the honor of staying in the stronghold, as tradition dictated.

However, many of her enemies also resided within the caverns of the stronghold. With so few warriors around during the day, Sáerlaith often felt vulnerable. This day, she sat at her desk in her main office, shifting through scrolls, when she sensed movement in the distance.

Sáerlaith pushed back her fear that her enemies would soon be upon her and then concentrated on identifying the source of the movement. She inhaled and discerned the presence of Máire and Marcus approaching, so Sáerlaith began to relax. She set down her scrolls and wondered as to why they would both be approaching her offices at this late hour. She soon heard a knock. "Enter," she called.

Máire must be returning from her mission, but why is Marcus with her?

Marcus walked in first, and then he pulled in Máire behind him. His stern expression surprised Sáerlaith, and then she scrutinized Máire, who swiped away dried tears with her sleeves, but otherwise, she appeared to be calm.

Their faces… Something must have gone horribly wrong.

Sáerlaith took in a breath to steady herself, willing her demeanor to be pleasant. "Is it done?" she asked.

"Aisling lives," Marcus answered.

She felt stunned and could not reply to that declaration.

Máire opened her mouth but also said nothing.

Marcus spoke next, and his words caused lightning to course down her spine. "Aisling knows that you ordered her death. She was prepared for Máire."

Máire's eyes shifted, but she would not look Sáerlaith in the eyes.

Only Marcus seems to demand my notice. But… Aisling lives? How could this be? Máire should have killed her… unless her doubts were as great as Marcus', or mine. Oh Goddess, what have I done? I must act.

Sáerlaith opened her mouth to speak, when Marcus cut her off.

"I'm afraid further questions must wait. We must take swift action. We all know that Aisling would have told many others, by now." Marcus beckoned for both Sáerlaith and Máire to embrace so they could whisper to one another without eavesdroppers listening in.

Sáerlaith left her chair, walked over to the other two blood-drinkers, and embraced them. She considered their options for a moment before proceeding to speak. "Listen carefully," she whispered. "You are not safe, here. Neither am I, but do not worry. I know what must be done. I want you two to leave Ard Mhacha. You will return to your quarters and pack lightly. Then you will go to the east to my home in Ard Ghlais near the coast as soon as the sun sets. Do you remember where that is, Marcus?"

"Yes," Marcus whispered.

"If you sense a Deargh Du other than me or Caoimhín, they will be your assassins," warned Sáerlaith.

"Can't we stay to help?" Máire offered.

Máire has failed. I can not trust her to stay and 'help'.

In response to Máire's offer, Sáerlaith glared at the youngling. "I think you have done enough!" she accused but then instantly regretted it.

I, not Máire, have created this problem on my own. Now I worry about the consequences that Morrigan mentioned.

"I am sorry," she explained in a whispered tone. "You were only following instructions, my instructions. I am more to blame than are you. I will do what I must to make amends." Sáerlaith found herself dreading what she needed to do, but she managed to push aside those notions. "You must go quickly. Caoimhín or I will join you as soon as possible."

Marcus nodded and said, "Very well."

Máire looked back at Sáerlaith and said, "Please forgive me." She then loosed her grip on the other Deargh Du and lowered herself into a kneeling position.

Sáerlaith reached down and pulled Máire back to her feet.

Marcus joined in.

"You are forgiven," Sáerlaith whispered before kissing Máire's brow. "Now go, both of you."

Marcus grabbed Máire and pulled her out of the office.

With the two Deargh Du outside of the immediate vicinity, Sáerlaith returned to her desk and kicked the hard wall of stone next to it. She hissed in pain and then realized that she had broken a few toes.

Sáerlaith limped to her chair, sat down, and closed her eyes. She set her elbows on her desk and rested her head in her hands. She hoped to Morrigan that she could stop things before they got worse.

chapter four

Ard Ghlais, Éire

side from his carving, Máire noted that Marcus paid scant attention to anything else these last few nights since fleeing Ard Mhacha. With the exception of sneaking into the local village with her to feed, he would not allow them to go anywhere.

On many occasions, Máire had insisted on finding herself a grove where she could walk the mists, but each time, Marcus expressed several agonizingly logical reasons for staying indoors, including the fact that they were targets, and Aisling and her allies could hunt them down at any time. Yet, she still felt the need to escape, since Sáerlaith's home contained little in the way of entertainments and reading materials. Without an opportunity to immerse herself in a ritual or a craft, boredom brought Máire closer to insanity.

I can not escape the fact that I failed in my duty and that my death may lie beyond the doors of the house.

What really irritated Máire more is that since they had arrived, Marcus did not engage her in much conversation. She would attempt to chat and harass him with questions, but he would simply utter terse answers in reply. Máire feared that he planned to leave her behind, allowing the Deargh Du to hunt her in Éire, and there would be scant chance she could escape to the outside world, as she knew little about it.

Night after night, the only sound, besides the wind, the sea, and the animals, was Marcus carving his figure of Morrigan.

Máire stared at him this night, contemplating snatching the figure and his knife from his hands. She found she could no longer take the confinement, his lack of attention, and the sheer boredom. However, before she could do anything, Marcus stopped and began glancing around the room.

The break in the monotony startled Máire. "What?" she whispered.

"We have visitors." Marcus set down the figurine and his carving knife and then drew both gladii from the scabbards at his hips.

She reached for her own sword from her scabbard and prepared for death. Máire closed her eyes for a moment so she could focus her senses on the intruders. However, she could detect only one Deargh Du outside.

"It's Sáerlaith," Marcus confirmed, as he sheathed one gladius, but he kept the other one in his left hand behind his back.

A soft knock echoed in the room, and he walked over to the door, unlatched it, and then opened it.

Sáerlaith walked inside.

Máire watched as Marcus peered outside before ducking back inside. He closed the door and reapplied the latch. He then sheathed his other gladius, before rolling up his left sleeve.

"No, thank you," Sáerlaith said while holding up a hand, "I fed earlier, before I arrived here."

Máire studied the elder Deargh Du, but she could read little in the woman's expression.

"I'm glad I found you both. How do you fare?" Sáerlaith queried as she rubbed her hands together.

Máire held back many questions, such as how far behind Sáerlaith were their assassins, but before she could begin asking her questions, Marcus answered.

"Well enough," he greeted, before holding up his carving of Morrigan.

Máire could not believe Marcus.

Sáerlaith just arrives with presumably vital information, and yet Marcus wants to discuss his carving? Although I feel like screaming, I shall hold my tongue... for now.

"It's beautiful." Sáerlaith's smile lit her face. "You've captured the very essence of Morrigan." She continued to study the face emerging from the wood.

Máire had to admit that he had carved a striking likeness of Her, but urgency kept Máire from voicing her admiration. Instead, she cleared her throat and asked, "Is there any news from Ard Mhacha? Something, perhaps, about our impending doom?"

Sáerlaith sighed. "Some good, some not so good." She looked at them both. "Further retribution will not be sought against either of you, or against me, for that matter. I will be able to retain my position as head of the council."

"How can that be," Máire asked, "after what we three did? I did not anticipate forgiveness. I expected a reckoning. Wait... further?"

Sáerlaith turned towards Máire and stared at her. "We have not been forgiven. The other council members and I negotiated with Aisling to keep this matter quiet, but at great cost. Unfortunately, Máire, you will bear the majority of this cost."

"What do you mean?" she asked Sáerlaith.

The elder Deargh Du turned away to regard Máire's father-in-darkness. "Marcus, any wealth you possessed at the stronghold in Ard Mhacha now belongs to Aisling."

Marcus nodded his head.

Sáerlaith turned back to Máire, looking as if she might cry.

Máire dreaded whatever Sáerlaith was about to say.

"Máire, since you have no wealth in Ard Mhacha, your clan in Béal Átha an Fheadha will be forced to pay eric to the clans of the Deargh Du whose members you and Marcus killed. In addition, the council forbids you and Marcus from setting foot on or flying over Éire, unless the council specifically requests your presence, or if there is some other reason sufficient to warrant your trespass. Máire, this means you cannot return to your home."

Máire bit back her tears and closed her eyes, trying to deny and forget those words.

I can never go home? How can the council demand this of me? Restitution I can accept, but exile? Aunt Sive, Caile, Bearach, they all need me.

Anger filled her heart… anger at the council for punishing her, anger at Sáerlaith for asking Marcus and her to execute those Deargh Du, anger at Aisling for standing up to her and then for reporting her actions, anger at… herself. Anger at herself for committing murder. Anger at herself for failing to do her duty.

I deserve punishment.

Soon, she forced her anger to bleed away, only to be replaced by utter sadness at the prospect that she would never be able to see her family again.

"Can I still write my family?" she asked, trying to keep herself from crying.

Sáerlaith took her hands and looked into her eyes. Tears welled up in the other woman's eyes. "Yes, you may."

"Thank you for that, and thank you for convincing the council not to kill us." Máire whispered. She soon felt a masculine arm wrap around her, and so she leaned against her father-in-darkness. She glanced at Marcus' face, but his features seemed restrained.

How do you feel, Marcus? Why have you not said anything? Why are you not angry, or are you just hiding it?

Yet, Máire could find no voice with which to ask these questions.

"How soon do we need to leave?" Marcus asked Sáerlaith.

"Tomorrow night at dusk," Sáerlaith replied. "I must escort you to the coast tomorrow night. Where will you two go?"

Máire looked up at Marcus.

He shrugged and answered, "Home. Bath."

"I see," Sáerlaith said before closing her eyes for a moment and then opening them.

Marcus let go of Máire and then smiled at Sáerlaith. "Since you will need to remain with us, I offer you all that we have to give, even though we are your guests in your own home."

Máire watched Sáerlaith's features turn cheerful. "Thank you both. I am honored to be your guest."

Marcus and the two women stood upon a cliff top south of Ard Ghlais' harbor, overlooking the rolling seas, where they witnessed massive waves crashing against the rocks below sending geysers of salt spray into the air. In the distance, Marcus could hear whale song, whose low droning and squeaking, mixed with the roar of the sea and the whooshing of the wind, seemed almost comforting.

Almost.

With his mind set, Marcus turned away from the sea, anxious to confront Sáerlaith while he still could. He faced Sáerlaith to address her, but he decided to wait while she pushed away the hair that covered her face.

When she opened her mouth, Marcus held his tongue once more.

"My heart is heavy that you two must leave and that Máire can never see her family again," Sáerlaith offered.

Marcus could no longer remain silent about his concerns, yet he did not want to insult Sáerlaith.

What must be said needs to be spoken aloud.

"Sáerlaith, it pains me to ask this of you, but I must. You have convinced Aisling to spare us, and I thank you for that. I also understand that we must leave Éire, but it seems to me that forcing Máire's clan to pay reparations and banning her from seeing her family is unbalanced. You spoke of sacrifices that you made, but what were these sacrifices–"

He ignored her attempt to interrupt his queries.

"You and I should bear more consequences than Máire does–"

"I did bear more consequences than Máire or you," Sáerlaith answered in a pained yet stern voice. Her eyes became hard, and they penetrated his soul. "Marcus, I have been walking this earth for nearly two thousand years. In this long life, I have accumulated a great deal of wealth and property." Her tone became harsh. "All of this wealth now belongs to Aisling! The punishment against Máire was personal, Marcus. You escaped further penalty because your wealth resides outside of Éire," Sáerlaith explained.

Marcus tried to meet Sáerlaith's wrathful gaze. "I will pay for Máire's transgressions," he demanded. "She deserves to see her family, again."

Sáerlaith's features softened. "I knew if given the opportunity, you'd offer to sacrifice your wealth for her well-being. Unfortunately, Aisling knew that as well, but she would not acquiesce. She insisted that Máire suffer, but she felt that your service against the Lamia warranted consideration." Sáerlaith's words turned sardonic. "Besides, it was not you who had intended to sever Aisling's head."

Marcus studied the rocks beneath his feet.

Sáerlaith's answer, that she bears the brunt of Aisling's wrath, makes sense, as does her personal grudge against Máire. Nevertheless, why does my service warrant clemency?

"I somehow doubt that my service against the Lamia meant anything to Aisling," Marcus said aloud, though unsure why.

"You gave so much," Máire said to Sáerlaith. "I'm not sure what to say."

Did Máire not hear me, or even Sáerlaith, for that matter...?

Sáerlaith walked over to Máire and embraced her. "You do not have to say anything, Máire. I put you both on this path." She pulled Marcus towards them, and he joined in their embrace.

Marcus soon forgot about his question.

"I only wish that your punishment would have been less," Sáerlaith said.

"Were we wrong, Sáerlaith?" Máire asked. "Should we have not killed them?"

Sáerlaith pulled back from them and slid her hands down their arms to their hands. "This was Morrigan's path." As she spoke, she met both Marcus' and Máire's eyes. Sáerlaith's words rang with truth.

"Sáerlaith, forgive me for my doubts," he said.

She drew him closer and kissed him. Sáerlaith uttered a mirthless chuckle and then pulled away. She stroked a hand over his left cheek and whispered, "Marcus, I could never stay angry with you." She then stepped towards Máire and embraced her again.

Máire started crying.

Marcus felt shock at seeing these emotions from her again.

Perhaps she might start feeling sentiments and affections again, soon.

"You will be fine, Maél Muire," Sáerlaith pronounced with a smile before kissing Máire again. "Now go, both of you. We will see each other again." Sáerlaith backed away.

His daughter-in-darkness turned towards him and wiped away her tears.

Marcus took her arm.

"I've never been outside of Éire," she exclaimed.

Máire looks like a young mortal woman again, and I feel a strange peace.

He released her arm and reached for her hand, entwining their digits. "Just keep a hold of my hand," he told her. "I'll guide us across the sea."

Máire looked back at Sáerlaith.

"Farewell," Máire and Marcus said to her, before taking to the skies, heading southeast towards Bath.

Over the Muir Mhanann (Irish Sea)

Máire pushed back her hair with her free hand and stared at the sea beneath them. She felt rather insignificant and overwhelmed, a mere speck of dirt floating over a vast ocean. However, she also felt gratitude that she flew with someone who knew the lands and waters beyond Éire.

"Look ahead," Marcus advised.

During the course of our journey, his mood has transformed from somber to excitement. Perhaps he wants an excuse to move elsewhere.

His sudden announcement interrupted her thoughts. "We're approaching land," he called over the wind.

Máire looked below and saw land. "Is this Bath?"

"Oh no, we are not near Bath, yet," Marcus informed her. "This is Caergybi. We will pass over an old Roman fort and watchtower... there." He pointed to some ruins below.

She glanced at him and watched his eyes grow distant, as if he were remembering past glories, battles, or defeats, before looking back at the ground.

They flew in silence for another hour over marshes, forests, docks, and large buildings. Máire felt a little sleepy, before noticing that they crossed over a small body of water.

"There," Marcus shouted, alerting her. "That used to be the port called Abona. It has a new name now, but I've forgotten it. Beyond that port will be the town of Bath."

Máire inhaled in excitement as they began to approach buildings that grew larger as they glided towards them, well-lit with torches and lamps. "I've never seen such large buildings," she muttered.

Marcus pointed to the large structure in the middle of the town. "There's the former Lamia stronghold. Claudius thinks it used to belong to some Roman legate or governor before the Lamia took it over, and now, of course, it is my home. Hopefully, Leandros found people to help keep it up."

The building loomed as they approached, larger than the duns of the kings of Éire. Beautiful gardens and sculptures of people and animals decorated the outside of the structure. There seemed to be a garden within the interior of the building as well.

After they both landed within the courtyard by the first gate, Marcus walked up to a large door and knocked on it three times.

She heard a strange mechanism begin to clink, and with a great creak and then a sigh, the door opened, and a mortal with a torch stepped out and stared at them for a moment, but then his eyes opened wide, and he smiled an infectious grin.

"Master has returned!" he called to the interior of the house. The mortal looked back at her and continued grinning. "And he's brought a guest," he added. The man then approached Marcus. "General, do you need to feed?"

"Yes, my guest and I are very hungry," Marcus answered.

The mortal whistled, and then two mortal women approached them. One of them pulled up her sleeve and thrust an arm towards Máire with eagerness.

Máire gracefully accepted the gift and proceeded to drink. After a few moments of feeding greedily, she felt Marcus pull away her donor.

The two mortal women giggled before stumbling through the corridor, chattering to each other.

"Shouldn't we heal–"

"Later, later," Marcus said. "They'll be fine. Is Leandros awake, Bran?"

"I'm afraid not. He sleeps. Shall I fetch him?" Bran asked.

"Yes, I'm afraid I must disturb him. Have him meet us in my office. Also, have the others prepare the baths and find clean clothing for myself and for Máire. Oh, and send someone to find Mac Alpin and Claudius. I think they're still living near Abona."

"Right away." Bran left them standing outside.

Marcus took her hand. "Follow me, and I'll show you our home."

"Our?"

"Yes," he confirmed, after turning back to look at her. "This is your home as well... that is, if you wish to stay."

She thought of her home across the sea and of the promise she had made to herself to return to Béal Átha an Fheadha after completing her duties in Ard Mhacha.

Yet, that cannot be home anymore. Will I be able to call any place home?

As Marcus continued to gaze at her, his expression became worrisome.

She could sense that Marcus began to doubt his bringing her here, that she may not enjoy living with him in this large house, but such a conclusion could not be further from the truth.

This place put the exterior of her former stronghold in Béal Átha an Fheadha to shame. Few of the Deargh Du she met could be called friendly, yet Marcus' mortal servants offered far more hospitality than most of her own line. Soon, their friends Claudius and Mac Alpin would be joining them. If only she could see her family again, but perhaps such a thing could be possible.

Máire wrapped Marcus in an intimate embrace and kissed him for several seconds. Soon, she could feel his positive demeanor returning.

Yes, this is my new home.

She released him from her kiss and cried, "It is good to be home."

epilogue

Bath, Bryttania

Dear aunt,

You must be surprised to hear from me so soon after my last letter. Though the circumstances surrounding my leaving Éire were forced, I've come to appreciate the wonders of this new home to the east. We, that is Marcus and I, have traveled the great forestlands and pastures, craggy peaks, fishing villages, ports, and great cities, the likes of which cannot be found in Éire. This beauty has lifted my spirits. This land is now my home.

In a strange way, I wish Marcus had brought me here earlier. Éire is beautiful, but most of our kind dislike us. I wish I could return to Béal Átha an Fheadha, but I'm certain the Deargh Du would enact further punishment against the clan for that.

Marcus suggested that we invite you, Sitara, and little Berti to join us here in Bath for at least a visit. He offered to send transport for you and your things if you wish to stay. There is a grove here that needs tender care, and I think that it might call to you. I know it will not be the same as the grove at home, but we both miss you, Sitara, and Berti.

I must warn you that Marcus' friends are staying with us, and they seem to have no plans to move on. Apparently, Edward burned down Arwin Mac Alpin's home, and Claudius complains that no place else in Britannia has proper baths. So, the three of them have joined us. While they are loud, annoying, and smelly, at times, Marcus is happy. I realize now how miserable he was in Ard Mhacha. Then again, I was cheerless and despondent as well.

To get back to the point of this letter, I feel as if my life is becoming more. I would love to share our home with you. I miss you greatly.

Yours in the Balance,

Maél Muire - Máire

continue the journey with...

dark alliance

morrigan's brood book iii

about the authors

Heather Poinsett Dunbar

Born in Houston, Texas, Heather began writing her first book at age eight. While her grammatical structure left much to be desired, she continued to hone her writing and storytelling skills. During a college internship in London, England, her curiosity about ancient cultures and mythology intensified. She backpacked through Europe, fell in love with Scotland, cried at the retelling of part of the Ulster cycle, garnered ghost stories from the Beefeaters at the Tower, wandered the Roman ruins in Bath, and danced around the stones in Avebury.

After spending all her spare time studying these new interests in many libraries and on the road, she began working on her masters' in Library science at the University of North Texas. She now resides in the Houston area with her husband and three cats. She loves exploring the local culture as well as the many Celtic festivals and events in Texas. She also works as a librarian for a local college and at a corporate library in downtown Houston.

Christopher Dunbar

Chris Dunbar was born in Greenport, Long Island, New York and then moved to Texas as soon as he could, at least that is the story he tells to native Texans, such as his wife. Chris keeps searching for ways to leave Houston, like moving to Auburn, Alabama, Dallas, and even San Antonio, but Houston just keeps reeling him back. Chris' day job is performing Business Continuity and Disaster Recovery, but his night job is coming up with creative ways to wound and maim the characters he and his wife Heather created. For fun, Chris enjoys the occasional novel and video game, but he also likes to delve into his Scottish ancestry and tool leather. When he can find the time, Chris pretends to play the Bodhran and the didgeridoo, much to the chagrin of his cats, Clyde, Brigid, and Maeve, not to mention his wife Heather. Chris is also an avid wearer of the kilt.

Published and Future Works

Title	Synopsis
Morrigan's Brood Morrigan's Brood Book I	Éire is under siege by blood-drinkers seeking a powerful artifact. The island's only hope is Marcus Galerius Primus Helvetticus, a former Roman general who once aided Gaius Julius Caesar in invading Britain but now fights to protect Éire. Can the Deargh Du ( ᚛ᚑᚂᚋ᚛ᚑ) rally in time, or will the invaders reclaim their lost power?
Rise of the Lamia A Story of the Morrigan's Brood Series	Marcus Galerius Primus Helvetticus, once part of Caesar's invasion of Britain, is now a Deargh Du with a mission to stop Gaius Julius Caesar Augustus Germanicus—known as Caligula—from repeating history. Infiltrating the Lamia in Rome, Marcus must avoid a former become his enemy, lest he realize Marcus is alive. Will Marcus succeed, or will history repeat itself in blood and conquest?
Crone of War Morrigan's Brood Book II	The Lamia (Λαμία) have forged an alliance with an Irish chieftain and his malevolent mother, gaining a foothold in Éire. With a massive army on the way from Rome, their conquest seems inevitable. Can the Deargh Du and their new allies thwart the invaders, or will their mistrust lead to their downfall?
Madness Short-Story	Madness overtakes one of the Lamia's most pivotal leaders after the events of 564 CE. Will this descent into insanity ignite a devastating civil war, or can unity be preserved despite the growing discord?
Reckoning Short-Story	In the wake of 564 CE, the Deargh Du must face the challenges of change or risk old strife resurfacing, which could shatter their unity. Will they adapt, or will past grudges tear them asunder?
Dark Alliance Morrigan's Brood Book III	A new menace threatens the Holy Roman Empire, spreading murder and chaos among both mortals and blood-drinkers. A fragile alliance between sworn enemies must confront this threat. Can they overcome their hatred, or will the empire succumb to darkness?
Curse of Venus Morrigan's Brood Book IV	The Strigoi (Стригои), cursed by Venus, ravage the Holy Roman Empire. Pope Leo III seizes the chaos as a chance to settle an old score with Charlemagne. Will their rivalry plunge the empire further into destruction, or can the Deargh Du angels intervene before it's too late?
Shards of Light Morrigan's Brood Book V	In the shadows, many watch as a dark alliance hunts for an ancient device to undo the corruption that plagues the Holy Roman Empire. But not all who watch remain passive. Will this unseen presence help or hinder the quest to restore the Balance?
Dynasties of Night Morrigan's Brood Book VI	For centuries, a brother and sister have manipulated two dynasties of blood-drinkers: Japan's Kyonshi (キョンシー), striving for independence, and China's Chiang-shih (僵尸), determined to maintain control. As their intricate game unfolds, will jealousy and vengeance continue to fuel this endless cycle, or will one dynasty triumph over the other with the help of an unexpected game piece?
Odin's Chosen Morrigan's Brood Book VII	Odin grants immortality to a starving king who seeks vengeance against those who condemned his people. Leading his army of blood-drinkers, the Einherjar (ᛖᛁᚾᚻᛖᚱᛃᚨᚱ), Runolf wages war on Britain, Scotland, and Ireland, unaware that other blood-drinkers inhabit these lands. Can Morrigan's Brood maintain the Balance, or will they be swept away by Runolf's wrath?
Hera's Wrath Morrigan's Brood Book VIII	In realms thought beyond mortal and immortal reach, dark horrors lie imprisoned, sealed away by the Tuatha dé Danann. Hera, Greek Goddess of Motherhood, holds the keys to their release. Will she use them to restore her vision of Greek family values, or will she unleash these ancient evils upon the world?

Title	Synopsis
It's In the Cards A Lusty Librarian Adventure	Cheri's mundane life as a basement librarian takes a wild turn when a professor and a collection of rare tarot cards and other artifacts enter her world. Join Cheri on a quirky adventure that defies the ordinary—because sometimes, even the quietest lives can be shaken by a little magic.
Bitches Love Unicorns Within *Dark Constellation: Origins*, Book 1 of the Dark Constellation Series	At a wild party, Kayleigh discovers unicorns—and other fantastical beings—are real. Bob the Unicorn sweeps her away on a magical journey through time, space, and realms unknown. As they dance through dimensions, Kayleigh finds herself falling not just for the adventure but for the unicorn himself. But as the night wanes, the lines between fantasy and reality blur. Even magical parties must end—will Kayleigh's new reality be as enchanting as the dream, or will she be left longing for the magic to return?
Dudes Love Faeries Within *Dark Constellation: Origins*, Book 1 of the Dark Constellation Series	Teddy, a pixie librarian, takes a job in the unseelie realm, hoping for fulfillment at Tír na nÓg's largest and most prestigious library. But his dreams are dashed when he realizes his new boss is evil incarnate. Demoted to the lowliest position of book-duster, Teddy and his inept yet secretly ambitious boss stumble upon a magical gateway hidden in the depths of the library that leads to ancient machines on another plane of existence—machines that could reshape the very fabric of the Otherworld. Can Teddy prevent the unseelie's malevolent ambitions from unlocking their power, or will doom come to all realms?
One Fat Witch Book 2 of the Dark Constellation Series	Hazel's topsy-turvy life in Houston takes a darker turn when her husband is kidnapped by a unicorn. With the help of a pixie hiding from an unseelie lord, Hazel must protect a key that controls powerful machines in the Otherworld. Can she save her husband and prevent a catastrophe, or will the unleashed magic consume their souls and plunge both worlds into eternal darkness?

Look for these Morrigan's Brood series titles by

heather poinsett ounbar & christopher thomas ounbar

there are more stories to tell, so look out for them

www.ingramcontent.com/pod-product-compliance
Lightning Source LLC
Chambersburg PA
CBHW020143150626
46552CB00021B/1407